Rita® Award-winning author Liz Fielding
"gets better and better with every book!"
—*Romantic Times*

Further praise for Liz Fielding

About *The Bridesmaid's Reward*:
"The characters are out-of-this-world fun, the scenes and
dialogue laugh-out-loud funny and the story is delightful."
—*Romantic Times*

About *A Suitable Groom*:
"A sparkling, bubbly romance with witty dialogue,
humor, and a deliciously scrumptious hero."
—*Bookbug on the Web*

About *His Desert Rose*:
"Once again, talented storyteller Liz Fielding
has given readers another truly remarkable tale of
love conquering all, utilizing intense emotional scenes,
dynamic characters, a powerful internal conflict
and an exotic desert setting."
—*Romantic Times*

About *The Best Man and the Bridesmaid*:
"A delightful tale with a fresh spin on a fan-favorite
storyline, snappy dialogue and charming characters."
—*Romantic Times*

Liz Fielding started writing at the age of twelve, when she won a writing competition at school. After that early success there was quite a gap—during which she was busy working in Africa and the Middle East, getting married and having children—before her first book was published in 1992. Now readers worldwide fall in love with her irresistible heroes, and adore her independent-minded heroines. Visit Liz's Web site for news and extracts of upcoming books at www.lizfielding.com

Books by Liz Fielding

HARLEQUIN ROMANCE®
3798—A FAMILY OF HIS OWN
3817—THE BILLIONAIRE TAKES A BRIDE
3821—A SURPRISE CHRISTMAS PROPOSAL

A Wife on Paper

Liz Fielding

CONTRACT BRIDES
From paper marriage...to wedded bliss!

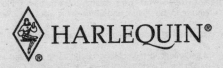

HARLEQUIN®

TORONTO • NEW YORK • LONDON
AMSTERDAM • PARIS • SYDNEY • HAMBURG
STOCKHOLM • ATHENS • TOKYO • MILAN • MADRID
PRAGUE • WARSAW • BUDAPEST • AUCKLAND

ISBN 0-373-03837-2

A WIFE ON PAPER

First North American Publication 2005.

Copyright © 2004 by Liz Fielding.

This edition published by arrangement with Harlequin Books S.A.

www.eHarlequin.com

Printed in U.S.A.

CHAPTER ONE

His brother was late, the restaurant was crowded, noisy, the kind of fashionable look-at-me-I've-arrived place he loathed, and Guy wished he'd made an excuse, stuck to his original plan to have a sandwich at his desk as he worked through the evening.

A rush of cold air as the door opened behind him gave him hope that his ordeal would soon be over, but as he turned he saw that it wasn't Steve but a young woman rushing to get in out of the rain.

She paused momentarily, framed in the entrance, spotlit by the bright lights of the cocktail bar against the darkness outside.

Time stretched like elastic. The earth stopped turning. Everything slowed down. He felt as if he could count every one of the raindrops sparkling in her corn gold hair.

It was tousled, as if it had been caught by the gusting wind that she seemed to have brought into the restaurant with her, stirring everyone so that they turned to look. Kept on looking. Maybe it was because she was laughing, as if running through the rain was something she did for fun. Because she *was* a breath of fresh air…

She lifted her arms to comb her fingers through her hair, shake it back into place, and the dress she was wearing rode up to expose half a yard of thigh. When she dropped her hands and the hem descended, the scooped neckline of her dress fell too, offering a glimpse of what the clinging fabric so enticingly suggested.

Nothing about her was flat; everything about her seemed an open invitation to his hands to describe her, to stroke the sinuous lines of her body. She wasn't beautiful exactly. Her nose lacked classical perfection. Her mouth was too big, but her silver-fox eyes sparkled as if she was lit up from within and the glow that emanated from her eclipsed every other woman in the room.

And, as time caught up with them, his body reacted as if she'd touched his personal blue touch-paper.

Pulse, heart rate, all the physical responses leapt into overdrive, but it was more than a lustful response to the kind of stimuli that probably had half the men in the room in the same condition.

It was like coming face to face with destiny. Coming face to face with the reason for your existence.

As he rose slowly to his feet she saw him, their gazes locked, and for a split second the laughter froze on her lips, and he thought that she felt it too. Then his brother was there, closing the door, cutting off the rush of cold air, breaking the connection between them as he put his arm around the girl's waist, pulled her close against him.

Something hot, possessive, swept through him and he wanted to grab Steve, pull him away, demand to know what the hell he thought he was doing. Except, of course, it was obvious. He was saying to the world—saying to him—this woman is mine. And, as if the gesture wasn't enough, he grinned and said, 'Guy, I'm glad you could make it. I really want you to meet Francesca.' He looked down at her with the look of a man who'd won the Lottery. 'She's moving in with me. She's having my baby…' Make that a man who'd won the Lottery twice.

'Mr Dymoke…' He started at a touch to his shoulder, opened his eyes to see the stewardess smiling down at him. 'We're about to land.'

He dragged his hands over his face in an effort to dispel the lingering wisps of a dream that, even after three years, continued to haunt him.

He straightened his chair, fastened his seat belt, checked the time. He should just make it.

Guy Dymoke was the first person she saw as she stepped from the car. That wasn't what surprised her. He was the kind of man who would stand out in any crowd. Tall, broad-shouldered, deeply tanned, his thick dark hair lightened by the sun, he made everyone else look as if they were two-dimensional figures in a black and white photograph.

The effect was mesmerising. She saw it in the effect he had on the people around him. Had to steel herself against it, even now.

She wasn't even surprised that he had taken the time from his busy life to fly in from whatever distant part of the world he currently called home to attend his half-brother's funeral.

He was a man who took the formalities very seriously. He believed that every t should be properly crossed, every i firmly dotted. He'd made no secret of his disapproval of her and Steven's decision not to do the 'decent' thing and get married. Demonstrated it by his absence from their lives.

As if it was any of his business.

No, what truly astonished her was that he had the

nerve to show up at all after three years in which they hadn't seen or heard from him. She hadn't cared for herself, but for Steven...

Poor Steven...

Thankfully, she didn't have to make an effort to hide her feelings as their gazes briefly met over the heads of the gathered mourners. Her face was frozen into a white mask. Nothing showed. There was nothing to show. Just a gaping hollow, an emptiness yawning in front of her. She knew if she allowed herself to think, to feel, she'd never get through this, but as she walked past him, looking neither to left nor right, he said her name, very softly.

'Francesca...'

Softly. Almost tenderly. As if he cared. And the ache in her throat intensified. The mask threatened to crack...

Anger saved her. Hot, shocking, like a charge of lightning.

How dared he come here today? How dared he make a show of offering her sympathy when he hadn't bothered to so much as lift a telephone when Steven was alive and it would have actually meant something?

Did he expect her to stop? Listen to his empty condolences? Allow him to take her arm, sit beside her in church as if he gave a damn...?

Just for appearances.

'Hypocrite,' she replied as, looking neither to left nor right, she swept past him.

She looked brittle. Insubstantial. Like spun glass. Altered out of all recognition from the vital young woman who'd changed his life in a moment with just one look.

Thin watery sunlight filtered through the October sky to light up her pale hair, emphasise the translucence of her skin, as she stood by the church doorway, shaking hands with those who'd taken the time to come and pay their respects. Inviting them back to the house. Cool, composed, apparently in control. The only moment when she'd seemed real, herself, had been that quick angry flush to her cheeks when he'd spoken her name. The rest was all just a role she was playing, he thought, a performance to get her through the nightmare.

One tap and she'd shatter...

He hung back, waiting until the others had moved off, before he stepped out of the shadows of the porch. She knew he was there, but he'd given her the chance to walk away, ignore him. But she was waiting for him to say his piece. Maybe she hoped he'd explain, but what could he say?

The words for what he was feeling hadn't yet been invented. The loss, the pain, the regret that the last time he'd seen his brother, Steve had been at his worst. It had been deliberate, of course. A ploy to make him angry. And he'd risen self-righteously to the bait...

Neither of them had come out of it with any glory.

But she'd lost the man she loved. The father of her child. How much worse must it be for her...

He stepped forward. 'I'm sorry I couldn't get here sooner, Francesca.'

'Ten days. Time enough to have got from almost anywhere, I would have thought.'

He wanted to ask her why she'd left it so late. Too late.

'I wish I could have relieved you of the burden of organising this.' His voice seemed to belong to someone else. Someone cold, distant...

'Oh, please. Don't apologise. Your secretary rang, offering to help— I imagine Steven's lawyer must have called your office—but a funeral is a family thing. Not something for strangers.'

He wasn't talking about the funeral, but the months before that, when Steve had been dying and he'd been on the other side of the world, unaware of the tragedy about to overtake them all. By the time the message that his brother was running out of time had reached him, it was too late.

'It took me days to get to any kind of landing strip when the message came through about Steve.' He sounded, even to himself, as if he were making excuses. 'I've come straight from the airport.'

Finally she turned to look at him. Acknowledge him.

'You really needn't have bothered. We've managed perfectly well without you for the last three years. The last six months changed nothing.'

Her voice was cold, too. Every word an ice dagger striking at his heart. But this wasn't about him. His feelings.

Right now all he cared about was her. He wanted to say that she was all he'd cared about for the last three years. Instead he said, 'Are you going to be all right?'

'All right?' She repeated the words carefully, as if testing them. Trying to divine his meaning. 'In what way could I possibly be "all right"? Steven is dead. Toby's daddy is dead...'

'Financially,' he said, pressing on, even though he knew that he was making things immeasurably worse. Or perhaps not. How could they possibly be worse?

Her silver-grey eyes regarded him with utter disdain. 'I should have known your only concern would be for the practicalities. Ensuring that I did it by the book. It isn't feelings that matter with you, is it, Guy? It's appearances.'

Which answered that question.

Smothering the pain, he pressed on. 'Practicalities have to be addressed, Francesca.'

Listen to him! He should be putting his arms around her, offering her comfort, taking a little for himself, but since that was denied him he was talking like a lawyer. If he'd been a lawyer there would be some excuse...

'Please don't concern yourself about us, Guy. By your standards I'm about as "all right" as it's possible to be. The house. Life insurance... That is what you mean, isn't it?' With that, she turned and crossed to the waiting limousine. The driver held the door for her, but she didn't get in, just stood there for a moment, head bowed, as if gathering herself for the ordeal ahead. After a moment or two she straightened, glanced back at him, then with a lift of her shoulders she said, 'I suppose you'd better come back to the house. For appearances.'

Then she climbed into the car and waited for him to follow her.

He didn't mistake her invitation for a thaw but he abandoned the car that had been waiting for him at the airport without hesitation.

'Thank you,' he said as he joined her.

'I don't want your thanks. He was your brother. I haven't forgotten that, even if you did.' And she shifted to the farthest end of the seat, putting the maximum distance between them, not that he had any intention of crowding her. Offering comfort that she clearly didn't want—at least, not from him. But he had to say something.

'I'm sorry I wasn't here.'

That earned him another look to freeze his heart. 'That's just guilt talking, Guy. If you'd cared about him you wouldn't have stayed away. Why did you do that?' For a long moment she challenged him. Then, in the shadowy interior of the limousine, he saw a faint colour smudge her pale cheeks before, with the smallest lift of her shoulders, she let it go. 'The cancer was virulent. Faster than anyone anticipated. I asked him if he wanted me to call you, but he said there was plenty of time.'

Instinctively he reached to hold her, comfort her as he'd hold anyone in distress, but her eyes flashed a warning. It was like hitting a force field at speed. Shocking. Painful.

He'd intended only to reassure her but realised that anything he did or said would simply fuel her resentment that he was alive, while the man she loved was dead. She clearly thought him capable of feeling nothing but guilt. And that only at a stretch.

'He was so sure that you'd come,' she said.

'I'm not clairvoyant.'

'No. Just absent.'

He bit back the need to defend himself. She needed to strike out at someone and he was a handy target.

If he could do nothing else for her, he could take the blame.

When he didn't say anything—and he didn't believe she expected or wanted him to respond—she looked away, staring out of the windows at the passing urban landscape as if anything was better than looking at him. Talking to him. Only a tiny betraying sigh escaped her lips as they turned into the elegant city street with its tall white stuccoed houses, where she and Steve had made their home.

The sound cut deeper than any words—no matter how much they were intended to wound.

The car drew up at the kerb and he climbed out, hesitating between offering his hand and the certainty that she would ignore it. But as she stepped on to the pavement her legs buckled momentarily beneath her and neither of them had much choice in the matter. He caught her elbow beneath his hand. She felt insubstantial, fragile, weightless as, briefly, she allowed him to support her.

'Why don't you give this a miss?' he said. 'I can handle it.'

Maybe, if he had been someone else, she might have surrendered control, leaned against him, allowed him to take the strain. But she gathered herself, shook off his support and said, 'Steven managed without you, so can I.' Then she walked quickly up the steps to her front door to join the subdued gathering.

Francesca paused on the threshold of her drawing room to catch her breath. She had never felt so alone in her life and, unable to help herself, she glanced back to where Guy was shedding his coat. For a moment their eyes met and she glimpsed his pain. But she buried her guilt. She'd meant to hurt him, wound him for staying away, and not just for Steven. Then someone said her name, put an arm around her, and she allowed herself to be wrapped up in this show of care from virtual strangers, no matter how shallow their sentiments, how empty their words of support.

But the imprint of his fingers still burned into her and she rubbed at her arm, shook her head as if to loosen the image. Forced herself to concentrate. This wasn't just her tragedy. There were other people here, people who needed reassurance about their jobs, the future of Steven's business. She'd left it to tick over in the hands of the staff for the last few months. Now she would have to take control, make decisions. But not today.

Today she had to lay Steven to rest in style, ensure that everyone had something to drink. Something to eat. Give his friends time to talk about him.

And avoid Guy Dymoke.

'Fran?'

She jumped as a voice at her elbow brought her back to the present. This minute. This dreadful hour that she had to get through.

'Did everything go smoothly?'

She looked down, made an effort to pull herself together. Put on a reassuring smile for her cousin. 'Yes. It was a beautiful service. Thank you, Matty.'

'You should have let me come with you.'

'No. No, really, I needed to know that Toby was with someone he loves and I didn't want Connie distracted while she was making sandwiches.' Then, with a little jab of panic, 'Where is Toby? Is he okay?'

'He was a bit fractious so Connie took him upstairs

and put him down for a nap. With a bit of luck he'll sleep through this.'

'I hope so.' Another hour and it would be over. Just one more hour. She could do it. She'd held herself together for so long. She could manage one more hour. She wasn't going to break down now. Not in front of Guy Dymoke.

Guy watched her as she took on the role of comforter, taking the hand of a thin young woman confined to a wheelchair as they exchanged a few words, hugging people, allowing them to grieve. She was the perfect hostess, ensuring that everyone had something to eat and drink, all the while managing to keep her distance from him without so much as a glance in his direction. As if she had some sixth sense that warned her when he was getting too close.

He decided to make it easy for her, seeking out those friends of his brother's that he remembered, catching up with their news. Introducing himself to those he did not. Checking the arrangements for the reading of the will with Tom Palmer, the family lawyer. As executor he would have to be there, welcome or not. More than that, he wanted reassurance that Francesca and her son were indeed 'all right'.

'You're not eating.'

He turned around and found himself confronted by the woman in the wheelchair, offering him a plate of sandwiches.

'Thank you, but I'm not hungry.'

'That's no excuse. It's part of the ritual,' she said. 'Man's natural reaction to his own mortality. An affirmation that life goes on. You know…eat, drink and be grateful it was someone else who fell under the bus. Metaphorically speaking.'

'In my case,' he replied, 'I suspect it would have caused a great deal less bother all round if it had been me. Falling under the metaphorical bus.'

'Is that a fact?' Her eyebrows rose to match her interest. 'Then you must be Guy Dymoke, the rich, successful older brother who no one ever talks about. You don't look like Steven,' she added, without waiting for confirmation.

'We're half-brothers. Same father, different mothers. Steve favours—favoured—his. Mother.'

'Should one speak ill of the dead at his own funeral?' she enquired, with a refreshing lack of sentimentality. Then, clearly not expecting an answer, 'I'm Matty Lang,' she said, offering her hand. 'Francesca's cousin. So what's the mystery? Why haven't we met?'

'There's no mystery. I'm a geologist. I spend a lot of time overseas in remote places.' Then, because he didn't want to elaborate on why he didn't include family visits when he was in London, he said, 'Francesca must be glad to have you here. Her parents live overseas, I understand.'

'They do. In separate hemispheres to avoid bloodshed. As for the rest of them, they're all too busy to waste time at a funeral that won't benefit them in any way.' She looked around, rather pointedly, then at him and said, 'It was one of the things Fran and Steven had in common, apparently.'

'I'm surprised his mother isn't here.' A B-list actress who had been through half a dozen husbands and lovers since his father had paid through the nose to be rid of her, she rarely missed a photo opportunity. 'She looks good in black.'

'She sent flowers and her excuses. Apparently she's filming some lust-in-the-dust mini-series in North Africa. She was sure Fran would understand. Call me cynical, but with Francesca getting top billing I suspect she decided there wasn't any PR mileage in admitting to having a son old enough to have made her a grandmother.'

'Not good for the image,' he agreed, doing his best to keep the bitterness from his voice. 'She was never cut out for grandmotherhood. Or motherhood, come to that.' Every time that Steve had got himself into trouble, every time he had sworn that this was the last time he'd dig him out, he had found himself rerunning a long distant memory of his stepmother screaming at his father, furious that she'd had to surrender some film part because she was pregnant. Had found himself remembering the miserable little boy sobbing his heart out when he had finally realised his mother wasn't coming back.

And he was no better. He'd walked away, too. He'd told himself that Steve didn't need him any more now he had a family of his own. But that had just been an excuse.

'I'm glad Francesca had you to give her some support today,' he said.

'She was there for me when I had my own close call with death-by-transport.' Her smile was slightly wry. 'Not a bus, in my case, but a combination of speed, black ice and a close encounter with a brick wall.' The sympathetic response that came to his lips on automatic was neatly deflected as she went on, 'Of course, since I live in the basement I didn't have to make much of an effort to be here.'

'The basement?'

She clearly misread his expression. 'I believe that Lower Ground Floor is the correct "estate agent" term. It's not as bad as it sounds, I promise you. It's a basement at the front, where I have my kitchen and bedroom and a front door for visitors who can handle steps, but the land slopes away at the rear. My sitting room and studio is on ground level so that I have direct access to the rear garden, the garage and my car. I can't walk now, but I can still drive.'

'I'm familiar with the layout,' he said, although her reference to a studio puzzled him. 'My maternal grandmother used to live here,' he explained when she looked surprised.

'Did she? I didn't know that it was a family house. I thought Steven had paid…' She clearly decided that she was getting into something that was none of her business. 'What I meant to say is that I'm not dependent. I'm totally self-contained and go for days without seeing either of them.' She stopped, clearly realising that 'either' was no longer a possibility. 'Fran managed to convince Steven that the conversion was a good idea. That a self-contained granny-stroke-staff flat would increase the value of the house.'

'I'm sure she's right.'

'She's more than just a pretty face. Of course I paid for the extension work.'

'Of course.'

'Are you sure I can't tempt you to one of Connie's sandwich surprises?'

'Who is Connie?'

'Another of Fran's lame ducks. She has a bit of

trouble with English and can't seem to tell her lemon curd from her mayonnaise, which tends to make her cooking a bit of a gamble.'

'In that case I'm quite sure,' he replied.

Matty grinned. 'Where's your spirit of adventure?'

'I left it behind in a steaming swamp. It needs a rest.'

'Fair enough.' Then, looking at the crowded room, 'Oh, good grief, this lot look as if they've taken root. I'd better go and circulate. There's nothing like a wheelchair to make people thoroughly uncomfortable, make them remember that they have to be somewhere else. And, if that doesn't shift them, I'll fall back on my pathetic-relative-from-the-basement act and dribble a little. I don't think Fran can take much more of this.'

For a moment they both looked in her direction.

'How's she doing?' he asked.

'What do you think?'

Francesca's smile was fixed, her eyes glassy with fatigue and the effort of listening to the two men who seemed to have her pinned in the corner.

'Actually, I think she needs rescuing.' He also knew that she'd endure anything rather than accept help from him. 'Who are those people? Can't they see she's at the end of her tether?'

Matty shrugged. 'I've no idea. Probably people Steven was doing business with. Obviously things have been let go a bit in the last few months.'

'Obviously,' he muttered, heading in their direction, furious with Steven, furious with himself, but most of all furious with them for bothering Francesca at a time like this. She might not want his help, but she was getting it anyway. 'We haven't met,' he said, offering his hand to one of the men and, as he took it, he turned him away from her, stepping between them. It wasn't subtle. It wasn't intended to be. 'Guy Dymoke, Steven's brother. I've been out of the country for a while. You're friends of his?'

'We're business acquaintances.' They introduced themselves, but he cut them off as they launched into an explanation of their precise connection with his brother.

'It's very good of you to give up your valuable time in this way.'

'No trouble. I was just asking Miss Lang—'

'This really isn't a good time. Why don't you give me a call?' he said, handing the man his card and mentally willing Francesca to take advantage of the opportunity to escape, but she seemed fixed to the spot. Beyond help.

'As I was just saying to Miss Lang,' the man continued, stubbornly refusing to take the hint, 'it's really a matter of some urgency and no one at the office seems to know—'

This time he was cut off mid-sentence as Matty caught him behind the ankle with her wheelchair. 'Oops, sorry. I can't seem to get the hang of this thing.' she said. Then, 'Fran, sweetheart…' It needed a second prompt before she responded. 'Fran, you're needed in the kitchen.'

'Oh, right.' She snapped out of whatever memory she was lost in and saw him. That seemed to do the trick. 'If you'll excuse me…'

'But Miss Lang, I really need—'

'Not now.' Guy softened the words with a smile,

all the while urging them firmly towards the door. 'I know Francesca appreciates your sympathy, but it's a difficult time for her. Bring your problems to me.'

Realising that they were not going to get any further, they took the hint and left.

'Jerks,' Matty said as she watched them leave, one favouring his left ankle.

'I don't think you're a very nice person, Matty Lang.'

'Really?' She grinned. 'That's the nicest thing anyone has said to me in ages. For some reason, because I'm confined to a wheelchair, people seem to think I should have suddenly been transformed into a saint.' Then, 'Can I leave you to mop up the stragglers while I go and rustle up a pot of tea?'

No one needed her in the kitchen, although she was just in time to prevent Connie from loading crystal glasses into the dishwasher. Matty had simply been giving her a chance to escape, Fran realised belatedly. Guy, too, although it hurt to acknowledge that he might have even one kind bone in his body.

She should go back. People would be leaving, but she couldn't face the drawing room again. The polite condolences which, for the most part, simply masked the unasked questions she could see in everyone's eyes. They were sorry Steven was dead, sympathetic, but their concerns were with the future. Would the company go on? Would they have their jobs at the end of the month? Survival was the name of the game. For them, just as much as those two tactless imbeciles who undoubtedly wanted to know when their bills would be paid.

Questions to which she had no answers.

It occurred to her that she was now the owner of a business that she knew next to nothing about. She'd talked about going back to work once she'd had Toby, but Steven had insisted that she had enough to do running their home, being Toby's mother. That it was his job to take care of them.

Even while he was dying he'd insisted that he'd got it sorted…that he was going to take care of them all.

She choked back a sob as she sank on to the saggy old sofa that filled one corner of the kitchen, curling up into it for comfort. For endless days she'd been holding on, knowing that once the funeral was over she would have to confront the future. But not now. Not today.

Guy shut the door on the last of the mourners, then went through to the kitchen to find Francesca. He had no illusions about his reception, but he had to convince her that she must call him if she had any problems. That he'd be there for her. He doubted that she'd ask him for help, but he'd leave his number with Matty anyway. She was sharp enough to call him if…

A ball bounced at his feet and he turned to confront a small boy who was standing on the half-landing. There was no mistaking who he was. He had something of Steve about him, a nose that was a gift from his grandfather, his mother's corn-gold hair.

The wrench at his heartstrings was so unexpected, so painful, that for a moment he clutched his fist to his chest as if to hold his heart in place. When he'd read that Francesca and Steve had a son he had been bombarded with such a mixture of emotions that he hadn't known what to do with himself. The truth was that there was nothing to do. Only endure.

He bent to pick up the ball but for a moment couldn't speak, just stood there, holding it.

The child bounced down the stairs one step at a time, then, suddenly shy, stopped about halfway. Guy swallowed, tried to form the words, finally managed, 'Hello, Toby.'

'Who are you?' he said, hanging on to the banister rail as he hopped down another step. 'How do you know my name?'

He'd read it in a newspaper clipping sent to him by his secretary.

Francesca Lang and Steven Dymoke are pleased to announce the birth of their son Tobias Lang Dymoke.

He'd sent the antique silver rattle, a family heirloom that should have been passed to his own firstborn. A gesture that was meant to say to Steve that he was valued. That they were equals. He'd hoped that with a woman like Francesca at his side, with the birth of his son, Steve might have discovered an inner strength, self-confidence to finally realise that. Maybe he had, but his gift had been returned. The message was clear. Keep away.

'I'm your Uncle Guy.' He offered the child the ball

and he descended another couple of steps until they were at the same eye level. Then, as he made a grab for the ball, he lost his balance and Guy found himself with an armful of small boy.

'What are you doing?'

Francesca's anxious voice startled Toby and he began to cry.

'Give him to me!' She didn't wait, but wrenched the child from his arms, making things worse as she hugged him tight, frightening him. 'What is it with you? You think just because Steven's dead you can walk into his home as if you own the place, pick up his son—'

'The boy overbalanced, Francesca. I caught him before he fell.' About to add that he was fine until she'd shouted, he thought better of it. She'd just suffered one terrible loss and it was only natural that she'd be protective. 'I was looking for you to let you know I'm leaving.'

'You've said it. Now will you please just go.'

Distraught, grieving, she wasn't about to listen to him and he wasn't about to try and justify his absence from their lives. 'I simply wanted to let you know that you don't have to worry about the paperwork, Steve's business. I'll handle it, and if there's anything you need—'

'You won't,' she declared, lifting her chin a little. 'It's my concern, not yours. And I don't. Need anything.'

Her rejection felt as physical as a slap. He took a breath. 'All you have to do is call my office. Speak to my secretary—'

'Your *secretary*? Well, thanks. It's good to know where I stand in your priorities.'

'I thought…' He'd thought that dealing through an intermediary would be easier for her, but the truth was that in the face of her complete refusal to see him as anything other than her enemy he felt utterly helpless.

Matty appeared in the kitchen doorway. 'I've made a pot of tea if anyone fancies a cup,' she said, then glanced from him to Francesca and back again. 'I can make that Scotch if you'd prefer?'

'Another time. I have to go.' He crossed to her, bent to take her hand, then taking the opportunity to slip her the card with his mobile number on it, the one he'd been planning to give Francesca. 'It was a pleasure to meet you, Matty.'

'Well, don't say it as if was the first and last time.'

'I'm sure Guy has more pressing demands on his time, Matty. A potential oil field or three needing his expertise.'

'I'll be staying in London for a week or two.'

'That long?' The scorn in Francesca's voice would have withered crab grass. 'Oh, well, then we've got absolutely nothing to worry about, have we…?'

She was near the edge of hysteria, he thought, and his presence wasn't helping. Maybe Matty realised that too because she caught his eye and said, 'I'll see you out.'

'It's all right. He knows the way. This used to be his house until he sold it to Steven at the top of the property boom.' He looked up and, seeing the shock on his face, she said, 'What's the matter? Did you think I didn't know how much he paid you?'

What could he say? Tell her that she was wrong?
That the man she loved, nursed, cared for, had lied
to her?

'He adored you, Guy,' she said, as he turned to
leave. 'Worshipped you. He was always making excuses for you. In his eyes you could do no wrong…'

How he wished that was true, but wishing helped
no one. Instead, he smiled at the child who had
stopped crying and was peering up at him from beneath long wet lashes.

'Goodbye, Toby,' he said, through what felt like a
rock in his throat, and the child thrust the ball he was
still holding towards him.

He didn't know what was expected of him and he
got no help from Francesca. Feeling helpless was becoming repetitive. He wasn't used to it. He didn't like
it. Choosing action, he took the ball and said, 'Thank
you, Toby.' The child buried his head in his mother's
shoulder.

'I'll call you tomorrow, Francesca.'

'Don't bother.' She didn't wait to see how he reacted. She swept from the hall, taking Toby with her,
and he forced his unwilling feet towards the door.

'Shall I leave this with you?' he asked, offering the
ball to Matty.

'Toby gave it to you because he wants you to come
back,' she said.

'His mother doesn't feel the same way.'

'Possibly not, but I don't see anyone else crossing
continents and oceans to be at her side—'

'Steve was my brother,' he said.

'—or leaping to her rescue when she was being

hounded by men anxious about their invoices,' she continued as if he hadn't interrupted. Her face, thin, plainly marked with everything she'd suffered, was bright with intelligence and he sensed an ally.

'Have they reason to be?' he asked. 'Anxious?'

'Steven didn't confide in me but he hasn't been in any state to run the business himself for the last six months.'

'I wish she'd let me know.'

'He wouldn't let her. At the end she called your office anyway, but it was too late. All you can do now, Mr Knight Errant, is stick around and help her pick up the pieces.'

CHAPTER TWO

FRANCESCA was shaking so badly that she had to sit down before her legs gave way. Toby struggled to free himself, but she clutched at him as if he was the only thing standing between her and some dark chasm that yawned in front of her.

She'd been so sure that Guy wouldn't come today. It had been pure relief when his secretary rang to tell her that although she'd finally managed to get the news to him he was unlikely to make it home in time, even for the funeral. Easy enough to assure the woman that she understood, decline all offers of assistance.

She should have known he would move heaven and earth. Steven had once told her that his brother was a man who simply refused to contemplate the impossible, that only once had he backed down, retreated from the challenge to get what he wanted. Guy Dymoke was a dark, unseen shadow that had seemed to haunt Steven. She should have, could have, done something to change that, she thought guiltily. Made an effort to bridge the gulf that had opened up between them, but an uneasy sense of self-preservation had warned her to leave well alone.

'Why don't you go and put your feet up, Fran? You look done in.'

Grateful to Matty for distracting her, she finally allowed Toby to escape. The one thing she mustn't become was a clinging mother, weeping over her child. 'I'm fine, really. Where's Connie?'

'She's tidying up the drawing room.'

'You've both been wonderful. I don't know what I'd have done without you.'

'I wish I could say that the worst is over.'

'It is. I just have to see the solicitor tomorrow. Sort out the will.' She didn't anticipate any difficulty. Steven had told her that he'd made sure she and Toby were taken care of; he must have known he was dying then, despite the fact that neither of them had ever acknowledged it and she had to believe he meant it.

Her real problem was his business. What was going to happen to that?

'Just remember that you're not alone,' Matty continued, distracting her. 'I'm here, and Connie will hold the fort with Toby—'

'It's not necessary, really.' She'd been forcing her mouth into a smile, her voice into soothing tones of reassurance for so long that it did it on automatic. But she was determined not to worry Matty. She'd made an amazing recovery but she was still far from strong.

'She wants to help, Fran. To be honest I think she's terrified you'll move away and won't take her with you.'

'No! I couldn't... I wouldn't...' Even as she said it she realised that Matty was appealing for reassurance too. 'She's family,' she said.

'Of course she is. That's what I told her. And Guy Dymoke looks like the kind of man a woman in trouble could lean on.' Then, while she was still trying to get her head around the idea of leaning on Guy, 'Is there going to be trouble?'

Francesca was drained, exhausted, tired to the

bone, but it wasn't over yet and she forced the smile into a grin. 'Are you kidding? I've got a company to run and the most challenging thing I've had to think about for the last three years is the menu for the next dinner party. That sounds like enough trouble for anyone.'

'Don't undersell yourself, Fran.' Matty reached out, took her hand, held it for a moment. Then, 'I need to know. Is there going to be *trouble*?'

She wanted to say no. Absolutely not. The way she had to Guy. But she'd encouraged her cousin to come and share the house after her accident. Steven hadn't been wildly keen, but the house was huge, far too big for the three of them. Matty had needed to be in London for treatment, needed to have someone close she could call on in an emergency, and there was no one else. Nowhere else. And it wasn't a one way bargain. She was company during Steven's absences abroad seeking out the merchandise he imported.

The truth was, she just didn't know. Steven had never talked about the business. Had always brushed aside her interest, her questions, as something she needn't bother her head about, until she'd stopped bothering to ask. She wished she hadn't allowed herself to be so easily distracted, but he obviously hadn't wanted her involved, and she had Toby and Matty...

'I don't want to think about it,' she said. 'Not today. Let's have that Scotch.'

'But what about the house?'

She heard the fear and knew it was a fair question. Matty had an investment in the house. She'd spent her own money on the conversion of the lower ground floor into a self-contained flat suitable for her wheelchair. A talented illustrator, she'd extended it to make a studio so that she could work there.

'He always promised me that the house was safe.' Always promised that he would never use their home to raise finance. She wanted to believe that he had meant that, but if the company was in any kind of trouble—and what company wasn't these days?—and the bank wanted its pound of flesh...

She and Toby could live anywhere, but Matty would never be able to find another home in London. Not like the one she had with them, especially converted to her needs. With the space. Room for her drawing board...

'I'm sorry. Of course he did. It was your palace—he said so often enough, and you were his princess.' Matty looked around. 'I wonder how he raised enough cash to buy it at the top of the property boom?'

'He didn't have to. His father left him some money. Nothing like the fortune Guy had in trust from his mother, of course—especially after some City fraud put a major dent in the family finances—but there was enough for this house. He just wanted everything to be perfect for me.'

As if he had something to prove. There had only ever been one person he needed to prove himself to—and, torn between relief and fury that Guy had never bothered to show up and be impressed by his success, she declared, 'And it was. Perfect.'

But she couldn't quite meet Matty's eye as she said it.

Guy paid the cab driver, peeled off the parking ticket stuck to his windscreen, tossed it into the glove box

and headed for the echoing space of the Thames-side
loft apartment that he'd lavished time and money on,
but which only served to remind him of the emptiness
at the heart of his life.

He poured Scotch into a glass, sank into the comfort of a soft leather armchair and stared out across
the river. He wasn't seeing the boats, didn't notice
the lights that were coming on as dusk settled over
the city, blurring the familiar skyline. All he could
see was Francesca Lang. Not sombre in black with
her hair coiled up off her neck, but the way she'd
looked the first time he'd set eyes on her.

He sipped the whisky, but its heat didn't warm him.
There was nothing in the world that could warm him
other than the arms of a woman who was forbidden
him in every code he lived by. A woman who today
had looked at him as if he was something that had
crawled out from under a stone. He'd anticipated a
frosty reception, but he hadn't anticipated this level
of animosity. Every single word she'd uttered had felt
like a blow. He'd been taking them from her all afternoon and he felt bruised to the bone.

He abandoned the whisky—there was no help for
what ailed him in a bottle—got up and walked rest-
lessly across to the window, seeking distraction.
Finding none.

He leaned his forehead against the cool glass,
closed his eyes. Running the endless loop of memory
that was all he had of her.

If he'd had any idea what was coming he'd have
been on his guard, but the moment Francesca had
appeared in the doorway of that restaurant she'd sto-
len his wits as well as what passed for his heart, blind-
siding him, so that he'd been exposed, vulnerable, and

Steve—clever Steve—had instantly picked up the signals and positively revelled in the fact that, for the first time in his life, he had something that his half-brother wanted, something he could never have.

He hadn't blamed him for that. He had just wanted to be somewhere else, a million miles from the restaurant, but there had been no escape. There had been an entire evening to get through first and all he could do was pull down the mental shutters, shake Steve's hand, brush Francesca's cheek with his lips as he welcomed her into the family, congratulated her. It had been a quiet torture then and the slow drip of it had never left him.

His mind, stuck in an endless re-run that he couldn't escape—didn't want to escape—continued to play that moment over and over every time he stopped concentrating on something else. Every time he closed his eyes.

The peachy softness of her cheek. A subtle scent that hadn't come from any bottle but was a fusion of her hair, the warmth of her body, her clothes, the fresh air she'd brought in with her, all enhanced by a touch of something exotic and rich. He'd had three years to analyse it, reduce it to its constituent parts.

All he had been able to do was wish them well, be glad that Steve had finally found what he'd always been searching for. Someone who loved him. Someone who would always be there. A family of his own.

And live with it.

Attempt to carry on a normal conversation.

'Where are you planning to live?' he'd asked. 'Steve's flat isn't big enough for two, let alone a baby.' It was like prodding himself with a hot needle.

'We're looking around for just the right place...'
Then, with a casual shrug, Steve added, 'Fran and I
looked at the Elton Street house yesterday.'

His heart missed a beat as he forced himself to turn
to Francesca, include her in the conversation. 'Did
you like it?'

'It's a beautiful house,' she said, not quite meeting
his eyes.

'Fran fell head over heels in love with it,' Steve
said emphatically. 'I'd like to come and see you tomorrow. Talk about it.'

He ignored the opening his brother had left him.

Maybe he was the one avoiding eye contact.
Avoiding a repeat of that moment when, with one
look, the entire world seemed to slide into place and
lock with an almost audible click; the kick-in-the-
stomach pain that went with the loss of something
precious.

He forced himself to look directly at her.

'You would like to live there?' he asked.

For a moment something shimmered between them
as, very quietly, she said, 'It felt like home.'

He dragged himself back from the edge. From stepping off. From saying, *Come with me and I will give
you everything your heart desires. The house, my
heart, my life...*

'Then I'm sure Steve will find a way to give it to
you.'

'It depends on the price. Unlike you, brother, I
don't have unlimited means at my disposal.'

'No one has unlimited means.' But he'd got the
picture. The reason for the invitation to dinner. The
last time he'd had a call from his half-brother—make
that every time he'd had a call from him—it had been

to 'borrow' money, on the last occasion to ask for start-up funds for his latest business venture. He'd assumed tonight was going to be more of the same, but clearly it wasn't to help with some half-baked business plan he wanted this time.

'Have you set a wedding date?' he asked, evading a direct answer and Steve didn't push. He clearly didn't want Francesca to know that he was asking for help with finance. But then why would he push? In the past all he'd had to do was lay out his desires and wait for guilt to do the rest.

'Wedding? Who said anything about getting married?'

'Isn't that the obvious next step?' He looked at Steve. A youthful marriage was the one mistake he hadn't been called to bail him out of, but anything was possible. 'Unless there's some good reason why you shouldn't?' He managed a grin of sorts. 'Is there something you haven't told me?'

Steve grinned right back. 'Relax, Guy. I don't have a secret wife or three tucked away. Fran's the only woman I've ever wanted to settle down with.'

'Then what's your problem?' If Francesca Lang had been his, nothing on earth would have stopped him from swearing his undying love in front of as many witnesses as he could cram into one room. Making that public vow to love and honour and keep her, in sickness and in health, for as long as they both should live... 'If you're setting up home together, having a baby...'

It was like poking a sore tooth. Something he knew he'd regret, but he couldn't stop himself.

'For heaven's sake, listen to yourself. Marriage is meaningless in this day and age. An anachronism.

Outdated. Just a way of keeping lawyers fat when it all goes wrong.'

He glanced at Francesca to see how she was taking that 'when', but she was looking down at her plate.

With no clue as to her feelings, he shrugged and said, 'I believe you'll find that even in the twenty-first century it offers some benefits.' What they were, beyond the special bond that swearing till-death-us-do-part vows to one another, he couldn't immediately summon to mind. But then that would be enough for him.

'The chance to dress up and have a party? I don't think we need to go to church first, do you?' Then, 'Look, you know the kind of nasty divorce Dad went through with my mother. Fran's been through much the same thing with her parents.' Steve leaned across and took her hand, grasping it in his, emphasising their relationship. 'We're allergic, okay?'

Guy fastened his gaze on some point in the distance. 'If you believe that not getting married will protect you from the fallout of a disintegrating relationship, think again. Once property and children are involved…'

'Guy, I hear what you're saying, but that stuff is just for rich people.' He didn't add …*like you*. He didn't have to.

'It's your decision, of course,' he said, wondering if Francesca felt quite as strongly on the subject—she'd remained silent—but he didn't dare look at her again. He didn't want to see the love shining out of her eyes. Not when she was looking at another man. 'Just don't discount it without real thought.'

'We have thought about it.' He lifted Francesca's hand to his lips and kissed it. Then, with a smile, he said, 'But if you want to play the big brother you can pay for the champagne.'

The message came over loud and clear. Steve was saying, This is nothing to do with you. It's my baby she's carrying…

That had been the only thing he'd been able to think about all through that terrible evening. Francesca was pregnant and he'd have given everything he possessed to change places with his brother. His career, the company he'd built up with a group of friends, the fortune that had been left to him by his own mother, just to be sitting on the other side of the table with his arm draped protectively over the back of her chair, knowing that the baby she carried was his.

Total madness. He'd only just met the woman. Had exchanged barely more than a dozen words with her. The briefest touch of her cheek against his lips. The moment she'd realised who he was, the hundred watt smile had been dimmed to something more reserved. Steve had obviously given her chapter and verse on all his grievances. Real and imagined. Told her all about his older, more fortunate half-brother who had everything, including a mother who'd loved him. Especially a mother who'd loved him…

It made no difference. Even the forty-watt version lit up his soul.

'Are you going to be all right on your own?'

'I've got to get used to it, Matty. Today seems like a good day to start.'

Fran smoothed her collar, regarded her image in the hall mirror. Black suit, perfectly groomed hair. Apart from the dark shadows beneath her eyes, she looked every inch the businesswoman. Steven would have approved. He had always said that image was everything. The trick was to ignore the butterflies practising formation-flying in your stomach; if you looked confident, looked as if you knew what you were talking about, people would believe in you. Okay, so it was three years since she'd set foot in an office, but her brain hadn't atrophied just because she'd had a baby—well, not that much anyway.

Right now a load of people were sitting around in the office waiting for someone to say, It'll be all right. Let's get on with it. And there was no one but her.

'I'll get the paperwork sorted out with the lawyers first,' she said. 'And then I'm going into the office.'

'What is he doing here?'

Guy had only just arrived when a secretary announced Francesca's arrival. She came to an abrupt halt in the doorway when she saw him, but there was no stop-the-world moment this time. No out-of-control hairstyle, no clinging dress to ride up and no yard of leg. And she didn't pause to look up at him with a smile caught on her lips.

He hadn't realised just how much weight she'd lost. Her hair was paler too. More grown up than the corn gold he remembered. Maybe that hadn't been her natural colour, either, but he preferred it.

That night she had been all vibrant colour, now she was monochrome, the pallor of her skin emphasised by dark hollows beneath her eyes, at her temples. It made the quick angry flush as she saw him all the more noticeable.

'Why is he here?' she said, ignoring him completely and looking directly at Tom Palmer, the family lawyer, who'd come around his desk to welcome her.

'Guy is your…is Steven's executor, Fran. It's his responsibility to see that the will is properly executed.'

Now she turned those lovely grey eyes on him. 'So that's why you raced back from the back of beyond,' she said. 'To secure your assets.'

'I have no doubt that Steven left everything he possessed to you and Toby. It's my sole responsibility to ensure that his wishes are carried out and I will do that, no matter what they are.'

Tom, who had undoubtedly witnessed family discord on such occasions many times over a long career, intervened with a quiet, 'Please, come and sit down, Fran. Would you care for some coffee…tea, perhaps?'

'Nothing, thank you. Let's get this over with. I've a full day ahead of me.'

'Of course. The will itself is a simple enough document.' He opened a file. 'First, Guy, Steven left this letter for you.'

He pocketed it without comment.

'Aren't you going to read it?' Francesca demanded.

'Not now,' he said. If Steve, the least organised person in the world, had chosen to write him a letter when he knew he was dying, he wanted to be alone when he read it. 'Tom?'

Prompted, Tom Palmer began to read the will.

While he'd been in a position to make conditions, Guy had insisted that Steve make a will in favour of Francesca. It had not been altered, and her relief, though contained, was nevertheless evident for those with eyes to read the small signs. The briefly closed eyes, the slightest slump in her posture as the tension left her.

'Is that it?' she asked.

'It's little enough,' Tom said. 'Unfortunately, as you know, Steven surrendered his life assurance to raise some capital last year.'

'He did?' The shocked words slipped out before she could contain them. 'Yes. Of course. He discussed it with me,' she continued, swiftly covering her slip.

That had been the other condition. The life policy. So much for his best intentions.

'When I asked if that was it, I just meant, can I go now? I want to go to the office, make a start on sorting things out.'

She was incredible, he thought. She'd just received a monumental blow but she'd absorbed it and, but for those two words, no one would believe it was anything other than what she'd expected to hear.

'Not quite all,' Tom said, clearly relieved that he hadn't had to deal with hysterics. 'I just need your signature on here so that I can set about organising a valuation of the estate. It shouldn't take too long.'

'Valuation?' She looked up from the document he'd placed in front of her.

'Of the company. For tax purposes.' She looked blank. 'Inheritance tax?' he elaborated. 'I did warn Steven of the situation when he originally signed the will. At that time there was no urgency, of course, but I did suggest he talk it over with you. Maybe consider going through the motions. Just a ten minute job at the local Register Office would do.' Guy could see that Tom was beginning to founder in the face of Francesca's incomprehension. Clearly she had never had that conversation with Steven, and he wondered just how many more shocks she could take. 'Just to satisfy the legalities,' Tom ploughed on. 'Perhaps after the baby was born...'

'Inheritance tax?' she repeated, ignoring the waffle.

'Is the company likely to exceed the inheritance tax threshold?' Guy asked, giving Tom a moment to catch up. Work out for himself exactly how much in the dark she was.

'I have no idea,' the lawyer said.

They both looked at Francesca for an answer, but she dismissed their query with an impatient little gesture.

'Tell me about inheritance tax,' she said rather more sharply.

'I don't imagine it will be too much of a problem, unless the company is doing substantially better than it was at the last audit,' Tom Palmer said, clearly unsure which would be preferable. 'However, since you weren't married to Steven any legacy will be subject to inheritance tax.'

She sat and digested this for a moment, then said, 'So if we'd been married I *wouldn't* have to pay inheritance tax?'

'No, but as I said—'

'And because we didn't go through some totally meaningless ceremony I will? Have to pay it?'

'Well, yes. That's the present situation, I'm afraid.'

'But that's outrageous! We've lived together for nearly three years. We have a child...'

'If you'd lived together for twenty-three years and had ten children it would make no difference, I'm afraid.'

After the brief stunned silence she asked, 'What's the liability threshold?'

'£250,000. After that forty percent of the estate goes to the Inland Revenue.'

'But…' Guy had thought she looked pale. He had been wrong. Colour leached from her skin, leaving her ashen. 'But surely the house alone is worth ten times that?'

'You don't have to worry about the house, Fran.'

'You mean the house is free of inheritance tax?' Francesca asked.

'I mean that Steven did not own the house.'

She shook her head. 'No. That's not right. Steven bought it from Guy. Three years ago.' She turned to him. Looked up at him. 'We've lived there for three years. Tell him.'

'There seems to be some confusion, Francesca. I don't know what Steve told you, but he didn't buy the house from me. It was sold to a property company about ten years ago, along with a lot of other property.'

'But he said—you said…' He saw her trying to recall the conversation in the restaurant that night. 'He was going to come and see you. To talk about it. He asked you. That night…'

'He asked me for help with a deposit for the house, that's all. I didn't know until yesterday that you thought I had owned it. And I had no idea he hadn't gone ahead and bought it.'

'But why would he need to borrow from you? He had money…' She stopped. 'How much?'

He didn't want to go there.

'How much did you give him?' she demanded.

'Two hundred and fifty thousand pounds.'

'But he didn't buy it?' This to Tom Palmer.

The lawyer shook his head. 'As far as I know it

wasn't even on the market at the time. He has been renting it on a yearly lease.'

'But it's our home,' she said. 'Toby's home. Matty spent thousands of pounds on the studio extension, converting the place into a flat she could use. If I'd known we only had a lease I'd never have encouraged her to do that.' She caught her breath. 'They don't know about that, do they? The people who own the house?'

'I would think it's highly unlikely,' Guy said gently.

To say that she looked stunned, confused, was an understatement. It was hardly surprising. He felt as if he'd taken a body blow, but she had been under the impression that she'd inherited a house worth upwards of two million pounds. Even taking into account the taxman, that would have meant she could sell up and have a million plus change to set up home somewhere else. Suddenly she owned nothing except a company that no one seemed wildly optimistic about and a short-term lease that might not be renewed. That she probably couldn't afford to renew...

Fran discovered that reaction was beyond her. It was as if she was under water, sinking very slowly, and she was completely paralysed, unable to do anything to stop herself from drowning.

One moment it had seemed as if she could relax, shake off the nagging sense of impending disaster. Now—

'There is one other thing.'

'There's more?' She turned and looked at Tom Palmer. Until now he had been wearing the grave expression of the average family lawyer. Now he looked positively uneasy.

How much worse could it get?

'The last time I saw Steven he asked me to add a codicil to his will. I had to tell him that it was a bequest I was not prepared to add to that document. We came to a compromise. He dictated his wishes to me and I promised to read them out at this point.'

'You mean after you've told me that my son and I are homeless and penniless?'

'Francesca—'

She glared at Guy, daring him to say another word.

'I'll read it now then, shall I?' Tom waited briefly, but neither of them said a word and he took a letter from the file in front of him.

'Before I start I want to say that there is nothing in this document that is binding,' he said, clearly unhappy about something. 'These are no more than Steven's...' He stopped.

'Last wishes?' she finished for him.

'Just read it,' Guy said.

'Very well.' Tom cleared his throat. '*Well, Guy, here we are again.* It's in his own words, just as he said it,' he explained.

'Tom!'

'Sorry. Right...

>   *Well, Guy, here we are again. Me messing up and you doing your big brother bit and saving my hide. Except this time my hide is well beyond saving. It's Fran and Toby who need you now.*

'Not this side of hell,' she muttered.

'First the confession. Well, you'll have worked this out for yourself by now, but I used your money for the lease on the house for some diamond earrings for Fran—since she didn't want a ring. Oh, and to pay the bill at that fancy private maternity hospital. Nothing but the best for mine. Something I learned from you. I just didn't have the cash to pay for it. But you never let me down.'

'He didn't have to do that!' Fran protested. 'I wanted to go to the local hospital. I could have lived without diamonds or any of the other stuff...'

Tom waited patiently for her to finish, but she ground to a halt, consumed with shame that Steven had taken money from his brother to give her everything her heart desired. Consumed with guilt that she had taken it without a thought. But that was Steven. He'd said money was something to be enjoyed. Spent it as if he never had to think about where it was going to come from. Maybe he never had. Maybe Guy *had* always been there...

Tom and Guy were looking at her and she lifted a hand, a silent gesture that he should go on.

'Okay, Guy, here's what I want you to do. Just about the last thing I did, before I stopped being able to do anything for myself, was to book a surprise wedding for Fran and me. A beach job in the Caribbean. It seems I was over-optimistic about my prognosis and I'm not going to be able to make it, but Toby is going to need a father and Fran will need someone to help her take care of her waifs and strays and, as always, you are it.

Tom says I can't make a codicil to the will leav-

ing Fran and Toby to you as a bequest, but I know you won't let me down. He's got the tickets, all you have to do is turn up and say 'I do'. It shouldn't be a problem for either of you.

    Steve'

CHAPTER THREE

THERE was a long, still moment after Tom stopped speaking when it seemed that everyone had forgotten to breathe.

Then Guy said, 'Is that right, Tom? You have the tickets?'

'Yes, but—'

He held out his hand and the lawyer reluctantly passed the travel folder to him. Fran watched in disbelief as he calmly opened it and checked the documents before turning to her.

'It's next week, Francesca. Is that convenient for you?' he asked. As if he was talking about dinner or a seat at the theatre and with about as much emotion. His face might have been hewn from wood for all the expression in it. His eyes chiselled from cold steel.

Confronted with so little feeling, something hot and painful clenched inside her and she recognised it for what it was.

Fear.

'This is a joke.' She looked to the lawyer for backup. 'This is Steven's idea of a practical joke...' If she'd hoped they would both laugh and admit it, she was disappointed. Tom looked down at his desk as if he wished he was anywhere else. Guy continued to look at her, waiting for her answer.

'Let me see.'

He surrendered the folder and its contents to her and she looked at them. Tickets, honeymoon suite, wedding ceremony. Everything was in order. Except that the name on the documents was Guy Dymoke.

'This is unbelievable.'

'It's a formality, Francesca. A paper marriage. Breathing space for you to sort yourself out.'

'I don't need breathing space. I certainly don't need you. I just need somewhere to live.'

'You and Toby, Matty and Connie need somewhere to live,' he corrected.

'Okay! Renew the lease if it makes you feel better.'

'I suspect that I'm going to have to do a little more than that.'

'You've done quite enough, Guy.' And she tore up the tickets. Once, twice, three times. Then she dropped the resulting confetti on the floor.

His head went back as if she'd struck him. Good. She wanted him to feel the heat of her anger. Wanted him to share the pain. Wanted him to feel...*something*.

How dared Steven leave her to his brother in his will as if she was his property?

How dared he accept the bequest as if it was his...his *duty*? Without an ounce of emotion. Everything locked down. Passionless. That was what Steven had said about him. That his brother never showed any emotion. Kept it all buttoned up. She wanted to grab him by the shoulders and shake him...

'Tell me what Steve meant when he said a marriage of convenience wouldn't be a problem for you,' he asked, 'Since you weren't prepared to marry Steve for love. Or maybe he was the one who didn't want to marry you?'

'What?'

Guy was so attuned to her, so aware of every nu-

ance of expression, the slightest movement, that he
saw the faintest start. Guy remembered the conversation he'd had with Steve that night he'd come and
asked for the money. It had been such an odd thing
to say; not about him—Steve had known how he felt
and was having his own private game with him—but
about her.

It was what he'd said… *'I've got everything you
ever wanted, Guy. And I don't even have to marry
her…'* Once the cheque had been safely in his pocket.
It was the only time in his life Guy had ever lost
control, punched his brother in the mouth.

Francesca turned on him furiously.

'Don't you dare blame Steven when he isn't here
to defend himself! This is all *my* fault. When he discovered I was pregnant he wanted to marry me,
begged me to marry him, but—' She stopped abruptly
and glanced nervously at Tom Palmer.

'But?' Guy prompted, demanding her attention.
And when she didn't answer, 'You wouldn't renege
on your principles, is that it?' he persisted. His tone
couldn't have made it plainer that he didn't believe
her.

She looked trapped. Hunted.

'Can we talk?' she said, her voice snagging in her
throat.

He recognised the turning point, the point when she
stopped attacking and went on to the defence, realising that she had more to lose than gain. With anyone
else he'd have gone for the kill. But he couldn't do
it to her.

'I thought we were talking.'

'Guy…' Her expression softened to nervous plead-

ing. In any other woman he'd have said it was an act.
'Please…'

Oh, hell…

'Tom? Do you need us for anything else today?'

'There are some papers I need you both to sign,
but next week will do. You are going to be around
for a week or two?' He glanced at Francesca, not
voicing the question that was in his eyes.

'No more,' Guy replied.

Francesca turned to say goodbye to Tom, but Guy
wasn't in the mood for such pleasantries. As she offered her hand, he grasped her arm and, taking her
firmly by the elbow, he headed for the door, not
speaking or letting go until they were out of the build-
ing and he had his car door open.

'Get in, Francesca.'

'Where are we going?'

'Somewhere quiet,' he said, 'where you can tell me
exactly what isn't Steve's fault.'

Guy hadn't had the first clue where he was going
when he pulled out of the car park, only that he had
to get away from the claustrophobic atmosphere of
Tom's office.

'The park,' he said. 'I need some fresh air. To see
something green that isn't soaking wet. To stretch my
legs.' He glanced at her and instantly regretted his
bullying tactics. 'It takes me a while to get used to
being in a city,' he said.

'The sudden change must be difficult,' she said,
quickly seizing the chance to move out of dangerous
waters. 'Do you enjoy working out in the field?'

'Enjoy might be putting it a little strong,' he said,
letting her get away with it. 'It's a challenge.'

'What'd you do? I have this image of you scrambling over rock faces knocking lumps of them with a hammer. I imagine there must be more to it than that?'

He could imagine her at a dinner party, talking to some tongue-tied man, trying to draw him into the conversation...

She was being polite. But she didn't actually give a damn and he'd have given a lot to be high up on some rock face, with the wind tasting of nothing more than the ocean it had crossed, instead of snarled up in the fume laden air of London traffic.

'It is a bit more technical than that these days. But, with all the satellite pictures in the world, you still need people on the ground.'

'So who's doing your job while you're here?'

She sounded as if she rather hoped he might have to rush right back. The sooner the better. Maybe taking off like that had been a mistake. The longer she had to think about her plea to 'talk', the more likely she was to regret the impulse.

'No one. Which is why time is in short supply.'

'It must be wonderful to have a real career.' A wistful note had crept into her voice. 'Be respected.'

'Being a good mother is the most important job there is.' It occurred to him that maybe she hadn't made the choice. That Steve would have needed a woman who would always put him first, last... 'What did you want to do? Before you met Steve?'

'Oh, I don't know. The same as anyone with a degree in Business Studies, I suppose. To find the next big thing.' She shrugged, as if faintly embarrassed by her ambition. Then, gaining confidence, 'Be the Amaryllis Jones of my generation,' she said, referring to the legendary founder of a chain of aro-

matherapy outlets, who'd just received an award in
the Queen's birthday honours list. 'Have my picture
on the front page of the *Financial Times*.'

'Then you met Steve.'

'Then I met Steven and got pregnant,' she said.
'Not much of a reference for someone who wants to
impress the world with her organisational efficiency.'

The driver of the car behind them hooted impatiently.

'Doesn't Amaryllis Jones have children?'

'The traffic appears to be moving,' she replied,
evading an answer.

He eased the car forward. 'Doesn't she?'

'Four, I believe. Look, you want to walk and I have
to get to Steven's office. If you dropped me here I
could take the Underground. It would be much
quicker—'

She looked at her wristwatch, as if to emphasise
the immediacy of her need to be there. She was definitely regretting her impulsive appeal to get what was
bothering her off her chest. He had somehow backed
her into a corner and she'd momentarily panicked.
Now she'd had a few minutes to gather herself the
last thing she wanted to do was 'talk'.

'You're going to step into Steve's shoes and run
the company?' he asked, ignoring her suggestion.

'Someone has to be there to hold the fort while the
future is decided, to reassure the staff—and the
bank—and to deal with people like those two men
yesterday, or there won't be a company for anyone to
run. As of now, that's me.' She lifted her head a little.
'I didn't thank you for rescuing me. Yesterday.'

'I didn't think you'd noticed.'

Her tense mouth softened as she glanced at him

and fell into a natural smile. If she was trying to distract him, she was doing a good job. He'd lived with this woman in his head, in his heart, for three years. He needed to remind himself that that was all a fantasy. That he'd been in the grip of an obsession. That he didn't actually know her.

Well, all that was going to change. There was definitely something not quite right about her relationship with Steve and he was going to find out what it was.

'What, exactly, does the company do?' he asked.

'Imports the kind of stuff that no one actually needs but most of us love to buy. After his last trip he was really excited about something. He said it was just ticking over for the moment, but that once he was better he'd really show everyone.'

'Everyone' being Guy.

'Maybe he left some notes,' Guy said quickly, intent on a little distraction of his own. 'Have you been through his desk? Checked his laptop?' She looked at him blankly. What was he saying? She'd been nursing the man she loved through a terminal illness. Going through his desk for business notes would have been the last thing on her mind. 'Has anyone else?' he said.

She shook her head. 'I don't know. I suppose I should have brought his laptop with me today. Some businesswoman I'm going to make...'

'Give yourself a chance. That you're even going into the office today shows enormous strength.' Then, 'We could look at it together if that would help?'

'We? Why would you bother yourself?'

When he couldn't be bothered to visit while his

brother was alive? The unspoken question hung in the air.

'I'm Steve's executor,' he reminded her leadenly, suddenly back to square one. 'I'm going to have to take a good look at the business. Sort out the best way to go forward. I'll need your input on that. If you're going to take an interest in running it.'

'It's all I have,' she reminded him. 'If I'm going to provide a home for Toby, I don't have any choice.'

'Matty doesn't pay rent for the flat?'

'Just a nominal amount,' she said. 'To cover her share of the outgoings.' Then, with just a touch of challenge in her voice, 'I suppose sub-letting of any kind is forbidden under the lease too?'

'Don't worry about it.'

'I don't think the landlord is going to be that re- laxed about it, do you?' Then, 'We'll need some time to find somewhere else. It's not such a problem for me, but it will be more difficult for Matty. I realise she's not your concern, of course.'

'Unlike you.'

'I am not your concern, Guy.'

He glanced at her. 'Shall we discuss that once you've told me what you weren't prepared to say in front of Tom Palmer?'

Francesca had hoped that Guy might have forgotten their precipitate departure from Tom Palmer's office. Which was pretty stupid of her.

As stupid as allowing herself to lose her temper with him. She'd come so close to blurting everything out, just to shut him up. Everyone in that room knew Steven had lied to her. Well, that was what he'd been like. He had been weak. Charming, but weak. But even when you'd known him you'd still believed him. Even Guy had been fooled…

Guiltily, she slammed mental doors on the disloyal thoughts. She had lived a charmed life. She'd been pampered, cared for, envied by friends who constantly worried about their partners straying at the first temptation.

She had never doubted that she and Toby came first in his life and now he was dead she wasn't going to keep quiet while anyone, let alone Guy Dymoke—especially Guy Dymoke—criticised him, judged him, blamed him.

She had been a fool to allow Guy to take charge and practically frogmarch her to his car. Except, of course, if she'd resisted, walked away, he'd have kept pace with her and all she would have been able to do would be hope for a knight errant—in the shape of a black cab—to swoop to the kerb and carry her away. As if that would have shaken him off. All he needed to do was go to Elton Street and wait for her to return.

She glanced at him. Having reminded her of the real purpose of this journey, he was concentrating on getting them through the traffic, taking shortcuts through the narrow little streets that connected the great arteries of London. His face was set, expressionless, all angles and planes that caught the light as they zipped in and out of the traffic. A long, thin nose that was a shade too large. The kind of cheekbones that she'd once seen on a Roman frieze. A mouth, full and sensuous and—

Guy brought the car to a halt, then reversed into a parking space.

'Oh. You've brought me home.' Then she realised why. 'You want Steven's laptop.'

'That, and it occurred to me that you'd never have managed a hundred yards in those shoes.'

'No, I suppose not.' She looked down. 'My feet are a bit small to fill Steven's shoes.'

He said nothing, did not move, did not even look at her. She swallowed, suddenly afraid. She knew that if he came inside she would have to tell him everything. That he would be angry with her. Would utterly despise her for the fool she was.

Well, that was fair. She despised herself.

'Guy?' she prompted.

He continued to grip the steering wheel. 'I want you to know that I loved Steve. He probably told you that I was an overbearing big brother, that I tried to run his life, that I had everything and he had nothing...'

A small, telltale sound escaped her throat.

'I was probably all those things, and yes, I did have an inheritance from my mother that left him feeling less loved, less important, less of everything. The unhappy truth is that he *was* less loved by his mother. That she didn't even turn up for his funeral tells you exactly what kind of mother she was. Non-existent. That woman doesn't have a maternal bone in her body, not an ounce of kindness, and I loathed her for what she did to him. I tried to make it up to him, but nothing I could do ever filled the void, the lack of self-worth, she left in his life. I hoped with you, with Toby, he might begin to find it.'

'So why did you stay away?'

'I was the one person who knew every idiotic thing he'd ever done. I'd been getting him out of scrapes since he was big enough to get into them. Always at his shoulder urging him to make something of his life like some nagging conscience.'

He finally looked at her and she felt the need to swallow again.

'And I was angry with him for not marrying you and he knew it. He said it was your choice, but I knew him…' Then, 'It's complicated.'

'Life starts out complicated and goes downhill from there,' she agreed.

'He was telling the truth for once, wasn't he?'

She didn't answer. Instead she opened the car door and swung her legs to the pavement and said, 'We'd better go in.'

She slid her key into the lock. Matty was downstairs, catching up with her work. Toby wouldn't be home from nursery school for another half an hour. She glanced at her watch and went through to the comfort zone of the kitchen, where Connie was getting ready to go and pick Toby up.

'Oh, Fran. You come home.' Then, catching sight of Guy, 'You want me to make lunch?'

'No,' she said quickly.

'I just going to fetch Toby. I take him to the park. Feed the ducks, eat ice cream.' Then, 'We could come straight home if you like?'

'No, you go right ahead, Connie. Have you got enough money?' Not waiting for an answer, she opened her bag, found a banknote and gave it to her. 'Just for emergencies,' she said. 'No need to rush back. Toby deserves a treat.' Then, feeling as if she had to explain why she was inviting a strange man into her home the day after Steven's funeral, 'This is Steven's brother, Guy, Connie. We're just going to look through some papers.' She turned to where Guy was standing in the kitchen doorway. 'Connie is our nanny, housekeeper, surrogate mother. I don't know how we'd manage without her.'

As she watched them shake hands she remembered what Matty had said. How worried she was about the future.

'Does she live in?' Guy asked when the front door had banged shut behind her.

'Yes. It's just as well the house is so big.'

She swallowed. Now they were on their own the kitchen seemed a lot less like a comfort zone.

'Would you like some coffee?' she asked to fill the lengthening silence. 'Before we start.'

'Why don't I make it while you go and fetch Steve's laptop?'

'You?' she asked, startled. Then, realising that she was as good as admitting that Steven had never crossed the kitchen threshold, she quickly went on, 'You mean you want to work in here?'

'I thought we could use the kitchen table. There's plenty of room to spread ourselves out. The study is a bit small for two people to work in comfort, I thought.'

'How do you...?' Then, 'Oh, right.' She kept forgetting that he knew the house intimately. But he was right. The tiny study tucked away on a half-landing was not big enough for two, not unless they were prepared to work very close. 'I'll go and fetch it,' she said quickly. 'The coffee is—'

'I'll find it.'

'Right,' she said again. 'I, um, won't be a minute. I'll just—' She managed to stop herself from saying, slip into something more comfortable. 'I'll just change out of this suit.'

'No rush. I'm not going anywhere.'

If he'd meant to reassure her, she thought, as she kicked off her high heels before picking them up and running upstairs, he'd failed.

Guy filled the kettle, found the coffee, and by the time Francesca had returned was pouring hot water into the cafetière. He looked up and saw that she'd exchanged her suit for a pair of softly tailored grey trousers.

Okay, she was in mourning. And she was three years older than that vibrant girl who'd grabbed his heart, but it was as if her entire personality had been toned down. Her hair, her clothes, her figure. She was just too damned restrained. Not a hair out of place, her make-up perfect. She looked nearer thirty-five than twenty-five.

Not that it was any of his business.

She busied herself with the laptop, all the time avoiding looking at him. 'The battery's flat.'

He searched the case, extracted the cable and plugged it into the nearest wall socket and switched it on.

'What's the password?' he asked, as the prompt appeared.

'Oh, good grief. I've no idea.'

He wondered if that was usual. Maybe. He'd **had** a couple of long-term relationships, but not **the live-**in kind. Not the kind where you'd exchange computer passwords. But living together for three years...

None of his business, he reminded himself again as he tried the 'forgotten your password' prompt, hoping that Steve hadn't actually taken any notice of advice to use something trickier than his son's first name. If it was numbers and symbols they'd have to hope that someone in his office knew it.

The hint offered was 'First Love'. He glanced at Francesca before he could stop himself.

She coloured slightly, but said, 'I doubt that I can claim that honour, and besides, I think my name would be a bit obvious, don't you? The first word that anyone would try.'

'Possibly. Could it be ironic? Some kind of food? There was a time when he would only eat Marmite on toast.'

'How old was he? Six?'

'Nineteen.'

Their eyes met and it was as if they'd both had the same thought. Steve, as an unshaven, scruffy student with no money.

She blinked. 'What about "Toby"?'

He shook his head. First love... And suddenly it came to him. He typed in a name...was offered the hint again. He tried it again without the capital and he was in.

'What was it?' she asked.

'It's "harry". All lower case.'

'Harry? Who's Harry?'

'He was a puppy Dad bought him for his fifth birthday. A liver and white springer spaniel. Completely brainless, but it was love at first sight.'

'He didn't... He never mentioned him.' Then her eyes dropped to the screen, as if suddenly aware that there were bigger omissions than that, and he wanted to reassure her about this one, at least.

'Steve never talked about Harry to anyone after he was killed. He just seemed to blot it out.'

'Oh,' she said, the sound small, little more than an expelled breath. 'How did it happen?'

It occurred to him that he knew things about Steve that she would like to hear. His childhood. Not just the scrapes he had got into, but the fun he'd been, too. He'd had charm, by the bucketful, even then. Talking, remembering with someone else, had to be better than bottling everything up.

'It was the summer holidays and we were at the cottage in Cornwall,' he said. Then, realising that she might think he still had it, 'Dad had to sell it, along with this house, when he had some problems a few years ago.' She nodded, obviously well briefed on how their father had almost been wiped out financially by the collapse of a bank back in the nineties. The strain had finally killed him... 'We were going down to the beach and Steve had Harry on one of those long leads that allow a dog to run without letting him go.' She nodded. 'You're supposed to lock them when you're walking on the road to keep the dog at your heels and, believe me, Harry wasn't the most disciplined dog in the world.'

'A bit like his owner, then.'

'A lot like his owner.'

And they both smiled at their memories of him.

'They were inseparable.' He paused for a moment as the sunny image of boy and dog filled his mind. Then, 'Harry made a lunge at a cat and it took off across the road in panic. He followed and went straight under the wheels of a car. The poor man driving it was devastated, but it wasn't his fault. He didn't have a chance.'

'Oh, poor Steven,' she murmured, and the hand that went to her mouth was shaking. 'Poor, poor love.' Until that moment, apart from the outburst in Tom's office, she'd had her emotions totally under control. She'd looked drawn and pale, but there had been no hint of tears. Now, as he looked sideways at her, he saw them well up, spill over and, without him knowing exactly how it happened—whether she turned to him, or he reached for her—she was in his arms, sobbing her heart out.

It was one of those bittersweet moments. To hold her against him with only the silk of her shirt between her back and his hands, to take the intoxicating hit of her scent, not in his imagination, but in reality…

Sweet, so sweet.

But to know that she was in his arms only for comfort because the man she loved was dead, that the tears soaking through his shirt and on to his skin had been provoked not so much by what had happened to Steve's puppy as knowing how much he must have suffered because it had been his own mistake.

He just held her, let her weep. He didn't say anything. What could he say? The empty comfort words… *There, there, it'll be all right…* The words people had said to him when his mother died and he hadn't understood where she'd gone, only that she wasn't coming back.

Nothing would ever be all right for her again. Or for Toby.

And he would have to live with the fact that it was his selfishness that had kept him and Steve apart for the last three years.

He'd told Francesca the truth. He had believed that Steve would do better without him around as a constant challenge, but that hadn't been all of it. His reasons had been darker. Less altruistic. He just couldn't bear to see them together. Had known that, but for the fact she'd been pregnant, he'd have done everything he could to steal her away...

'Sorry,' she mumbled into his shoulder. 'That caught me by surprise.'

'It's okay,' he said. 'Crying is okay.'

'It's embarrassing when you do it in public,' she said as she finally pulled back, not quite looking at him. 'I'm really sorry.' Whether she was referring to the tears or their unexpected closeness he couldn't say.

'I'm not "public",' he said, as she rubbed the palm of her hand across her cheek, sniffed, then looked around, as if hoping a box of tissues might magically appear. 'Steve was my brother.'

He wanted to tell her how he'd wept too, when he'd realised what he'd done. That there would never be a chance to put his arms around Steve and just hug him. He wanted to cling to her, never let her go, but he didn't resist as she pulled away, instantly releasing her and taking a clean handkerchief from his pocket. She took it, pulled a face that might have been a grin, or maybe just a grimace.

'You and Steven must be the only men in the world who still use linen handkerchiefs,' she said ruefully as she carefully wiped her eyes, blew her nose. Giving herself time to recover.

Unfortunately there was no such relief for him. He was beyond help.

'It was instilled in the nursery. Nanny was the old-fashioned variety. Starched aprons, two slices of bread and butter and all the crusts, if you wanted cake for tea. And bed by six,' he said, trying to make light of the misery of it. 'And reinforced at school. Boys always had to carry a clean handkerchief, a coin for the telephone and a safety pin.'

'Now all the kids carry mobile phones instead. What was the safety pin for?'

'I have absolutely no idea. Perhaps it was simply training for later life, although I somehow doubt any woman would welcome the offer of a two inch safety pin to rescue a snapped bra strap.'

She laughed. 'Oh, I don't know. In an emergency…' It was as if the sun had come out and cracked the ice. 'This would be boarding school, I take it?'

'It would. From eight years old until eighteen, and then it was off to university. My father came from the class of parents who knew how to keep children out of their hair.'

'It sounds ghastly. Steven put Toby down for Eton at birth, but I told him it was a waste of time. There was no way I'd let him go.'

'Well, I guess the difference is that Toby has a mother.'

'Yes, I suppose. How old were you when your mother died?'

'Four. She was thrown from a horse. Killed instantly. Steve's mother looked very much like her and I suspect she may have played up the resemblance. Dad said afterwards, when I was old enough for him to talk about it, that he thought because she looked like my mother she would be like her. He was utterly bereft, not thinking straight…'

'You had a lot in common. You and Steven.'

'You'd have thought so. Maybe if I'd been there for him, but I was already away at prep school when his mother finally left.'

'Finally?'

'She was never exactly a fixture. She'd hooked herself a millionaire with a house in London and a country estate. She didn't realise that he spent as little time in London as possible. She certainly hadn't counted on being a country housewife and mother.'

'No one seems to have been fixed in his life. A visiting god, that's what he called you. You descended on them during the holidays from Eton. Perfect. Unmatchable.'

'Maybe I should have made more of an effort to get into some serious trouble. Be suspended once or twice. He certainly found it easy enough when he followed me there.'

'Were you such a paragon?'

'No, just luckier.' Luckier all his life, until Steve met Francesca instead of him… 'I didn't get caught,' he said. Then, 'Why didn't you marry him, Francesca?'

She didn't immediately answer him. Instead, she carefully poured coffee into two mugs. 'Cream, sugar?' she offered.

'No. Thank you.'

She fetched some cream from the fridge and added a little to her mug. He sensed that she was simply spinning time out while she sorted out an answer in her head.

He didn't push. He knew she was going to tell him and he was content to wait until she was ready to talk.

She didn't sit down but picked up her mug and crossed to the kitchen door. It opened on to a small veranda created from the roof of the new extension to the lower floor. He'd need to get a surveyor over the place, make sure that it was sound. Check out the situation with planning permission. Somehow placate the owner of the house.

He picked up his own mug and followed her outside into the autumn sunshine. The veranda, a sun trap with a small table and a couple of chairs and pots overflowing with old-fashioned flowers and herbs, was a great addition, he had to admit. It was stoutly enclosed for safety and there was a gate protecting the steps that led down to the garden. The swing was new, too. And the brightly coloured garden toys for Toby to climb over and through.

'His birthday present,' she said, following his gaze. 'From Steven. We were going to have a little party...' She placed her mug on the table but didn't sit down. Instead, she leaned against the rail so that she had her back to him. 'It had to be cancelled.'

He felt he should know what to say. He'd been through this. Lived through this. All he could feel was pain that another child was going to suffer such an unimaginable loss. Vow to himself that this time he would be there. That he wouldn't let Toby down in the same way he'd let down his brother.

That was what Steve was asking him to do. Be there. And he would be.

Fran was silent for so long that he realised she wasn't going to be able to look him in the face, tell him the truth, whatever it was, and his gut twisted with the certainty that it was going to be something terrible. But Steve's features were imprinted on the boy. Unmistakable. It wasn't that. And he was at a loss to know what could be so awful.

Then she turned around to look at him and said, 'I didn't marry Steven because I was already married.'

And then he knew.

CHAPTER FOUR

As STUNNED silences went, the one that followed her confession was epic. It went on and on, stretching the air until she thought it would snap. That Guy might never speak to her again.

Fran didn't blame him. Saying the words out loud had been as shocking to her as to him. She'd buried the truth so deep inside her that for long periods she could forget those ten minutes when she'd stood in front of a registrar, barely nineteen, burning with ideals, going through a ceremony that had seemed meaningless to her. Marriage was an outdated institution. Just another way of controlling people, so why not use it against the system?

It seemed like a lifetime ago.

It was only when, pregnant with Toby, Steven had asked her to marry him that the reality of her situation had dawned on her.

Maybe that was why she'd told Guy—to expiate herself. She was never going to be able to put it right with Steven now. But his total stillness, total silence, was so frightening that she reached out, instinctively, to hold on to the railing and brace herself for his reaction.

Guy was stunned. Steve...yes. Marriage was the kind of mess he might have got himself into when he was younger; he'd actually asked him if there was any impediment to their marriage. But Francesca...

Questions piled in on him. Who had she been mar-

ried to? When? What had happened? She must have
been so young...

One question, the one he least wanted to ask—the
one he least wanted an answer to—pushed its way to
the front and refused to be brushed aside.

'Did Steve know?'

She swallowed. He saw the nervous reaction and
knew the answer, even before she shook her head.

He dragged both hands through his hair, looked up
at the pale blue sky, anywhere but at her, and blew
out a long breath that he must have been holding ever
since she'd dropped her bombshell.

'Well,' he said, when at last he could speak through
a pain that was slicing into his heart. 'He lied to you
about the house. I guess you're about even.'

She didn't answer. He didn't expect her to. There
really wasn't anything to say. He should walk away
now. Take the easy way out and protest the needs of
business. All she really needed was money, and Tom
could handle that.

But he couldn't leave it. Or let it rest.

'You didn't think,' he said, twisting the knife—in
her, or in himself, he'd have been hard pressed to
say— 'of getting a divorce? Or are you against those
on principle, too?' Then, 'Oh, no. Sorry. We've just
established that you don't have any principles—'

'It wasn't a proper marriage,' she said, rallying, to
cut through his vile sarcasm. But he couldn't stop
himself.

'No? Maybe you'd care to explain the difference
between a proper and an improper marriage to me.
These are not concepts I'm familiar with.'

She flushed, but didn't crumble. If anything she
stood taller... 'I meant,' she said, 'that it was in name

only. I married a fellow student when I was in my first year at university. He was going to be sent back to a country where he'd have been in danger.'

'But that's—'

'I know. Illegal. But his father had been murdered, his mother was in prison. He was desperate.' She shrugged. 'At least, that was the story. It took me a while to realise that it was just a racket. Gullible students hot on human rights issues who thought they were being noble were being used by people who knew how to work the system.'

It just got worse... 'Are you saying he wasn't a student?'

'I'd seen him on the campus. He knew enough to convince me that he was reading law and I had no reason to doubt him.'

'Surely you had to live with him? At least make it look as if you did?'

'Only if Immigration decided to investigate. I don't suppose they have the resources to investigate everyone, and I never saw him again once we'd parted outside the register office. Him clutching the marriage certificate to prove his bona fides to the authorities. Me clutching my ideals to my bosom, thinking I'd done something good.'

'You didn't think to go to the police when you realised the truth?'

'It took a while for me to catch on. He'd said he would have to go to London to sort everything out. That it would probably take a few weeks. It was only when he didn't return the following term and I was concerned that he'd been deported after all that I asked someone in the law faculty to try and find out what had happened. Of course no one there had ever heard of him. I'm not stupid—' She paused, gave the smallest of shrugs, 'All right, I *am* stupid, but I knew what I'd done was against the law. That at the very least I could be thrown out of university as an example. A warning. So I just put it out of my mind. Tried to forget it had ever happened. Told myself I'd clear up the mess after I'd graduated.'

Her knuckles, white as she gripped the railing, gave the lie to her apparent insouciance.

'I didn't, of course. I was too busy with my first job, too short of money to pay anyone to find him. Not that I had the first idea where to start. And it just didn't seem that important.'

'And then you met Steve.'

'Even then... Until I realised I was pregnant and Steven was so excited, wanted to get married immediately. I went to see a solicitor then, but since I had no way of finding the man I'd married I was told I'd have to wait the full five years before I could institute divorce proceedings without his consent.'

'Why didn't you just tell Steve?'

'You wouldn't understand.'

Understand? Of course he didn't understand! 'Try me,' he urged.

'It's difficult.'

'I'll bet.'

She looked a touch desperate. 'He worshipped me, Guy. Had me on this pedestal...' She looked at him. 'It's an uncomfortable place to be.'

'Especially when you don't deserve to be there.'

She flared up. 'I told you you wouldn't understand. But then you're comfortable up there looking down on the rest of us, aren't you?'

'I'm not...' He stopped. He'd asked for that.

Deserved it. 'Is there anything I can do to help? To sort it out?'

'It's a little late for that, wouldn't you say? But no. The five years were up this year. The decree was finalised a couple of months ago.'

The relief he felt was foolish beyond words. But real none the less.

She turned away from him to look out over the garden. 'How ironic that Steven should have booked a wedding. I was going to do that. Take him to a tropical island, tell him the truth... Maybe he found the brochure I'd brought home and thought I was hinting.'

'You were that sure he'd say yes?' he demanded brutally. 'When he knew what you'd done? Or maybe you were going to gloss over that bit?' And then, when she flinched, he'd have given anything to call the words back. Of course his brother would have said yes. Maybe even come clean about his own deception...

'Unfortunately there was no way to get around that word "divorced" on the marriage certificate. Besides, I wanted to climb down to earth. Ground our relationship. Think about having a brother or sister for Toby.'

The tears were close again, but she managed to hold them back as, with a gesture that took in the house, the garden, everything, she glanced back at him.

'That's what all this was about, Guy. He was so insecure. He thought he had to give me all this to keep me with him. It was a long time before I understood that. He deserved to know, to be sure that I would never have left him...'

'And now?' The knife was definitely in his own gut.

'Now?' Francesca released the handrail as if, having unburdened herself, she no longer needed its support. 'Now I think we'd better get back to business. I'd still like to go into the office today. I've got a business to run.'

She didn't wait for him to speak, but walked resolutely towards the door, leaving him to decide whether he would join her or not. He stepped back, let her pass, and then after a moment he retrieved their untouched mugs of coffee and followed her inside. She'd brought down Steven's large briefcase, too, and she started emptying it of files, notebooks, catalogues. Keeping her head down in an attempt to hide the fact that tears were running down her cheeks.

'Why don't you check the laptop?' she suggested.

'If that suits you,' he said briskly, as if he hadn't noticed.

She dug his handkerchief out of her pocket and blew her nose. 'I don't actually have much choice in the matter, do I? And the sooner it's done, the sooner you'll be gone.'

He was saved from answering by Toby, who raced through the hall and then came to an abrupt halt just out of his reach, suddenly overcome with shyness.

'I'm sorry,' Connie said, following him at a more sedate pace. 'He lost all interest in the ducks the minute he heard that his uncle Guy was here.' Then, seeing Francesca's expression, her face fell. 'I should not say?'

'No problem,' he said quickly. Then, 'Hi, Toby.' His voice was unexpectedly thick with emotion as he smiled at the child, wanting to sweep him up, hug him, but his long absence denied him that pleasure, that joy. He would have to earn his place in his brother's family and he hadn't made a good start. 'I didn't know I'd be seeing you today or I'd have brought your ball with me.'

''s'okay.' The boy took a step nearer, his eyes wide as he looked at the laptop. 'Can I play on that?'

'Oh, right! Budding genius,' he said, grabbing his chance before his mother intervened and sent him off for a nap—anything to keep the bullying monster away from her precious boy. Held out his hand in a mute invitation to join him. Toby didn't need any further encouragement, but scrambled up on to his lap. 'Right, Mr Einstein, this is what we're going to do. Since this fine machine has a CD rewriter, we're going to copy some files so that I can take them home to look at and leave your mother in peace. Want to help?'

'Can I?' Toby looked up at him with a wide-eyed wonder that tugged at his heart. 'Really?'

'Absolutely.' He took an unused CD out of the laptop case. On the point of giving it to Toby to hold, he spotted the state of his fingers and thought better of it. Instead he said, 'Can you press that button for me?' When the drawer clicked out he laid the CD in place. 'Now push it back until it clicks—gently.'

It took Toby a couple of goes to make it click shut and he looked up for reassurance.

'Good job. Okay, now I'm going to take your finger…' He took his tiny hand in his own and laid the end of his finger over Toby's. 'And we're going to press that key. Just once. Lightly.' He tapped the key with Toby's finger and a list of files came up.

'Oh!'

'You liked that? Want to do it again?'

After doing it half a dozen times they moved on, and between them they marked the files and copied them to the CD. It took longer than if he'd done it on his own, but that didn't matter. He'd wasted too much time, staying away, doing the right thing. This was the right thing...

When they'd done he looked up and discovered that both Connie and Francesca were watching them, apparently transfixed.

'What?' he said.

'Nothing.' Francesca swallowed. 'It's just that...people don't usually let little boys play with thousands of pounds worth of computer hardware.'

'No? Believe me, this was easy. Toby speaks English. It's a lot harder when you're in some place that the world forgot—or more likely never knew existed—and the kids only speak some dialect that has never been written down.' Then, 'And I resent "playing". We weren't playing, we were working.'

'Yes. Well. I'll, um, get on. Connie, maybe Mr Einstein over there could do with a nap.'

He lifted Toby down and said, 'Off you go, partner. Next time I come I'll bring your ball.'

'Will you play f'ball with me?'

Football. He swallowed. His brother might have protected his laptop from sticky fingers, but he knew that Steve would have played football all day with his little boy: he'd never quite grown up himself, after all. And who would be there for the child now if Guy disappeared back overseas, left lawyers and money to do what his brother had expected him to do personally? Care.

'I'd like that,' he said. And, when the little boy put his arms up for a hug, it was his turn to choke back the tears.

After Guy had gone, with Toby asleep and Connie tackling a pile of ironing, Fran determinedly ignored the faint smell of scorching and took everything up to Steven's office. She longed to just put her head down on his desk and weep, but what use was that?

Instead, she set about looking through the papers. What she should have been doing instead of watching Guy with Toby.

Guy drove to his office, dealt with the condolences, then worked his way through his messages. One of them was from the pair he'd met at the funeral. There was no point in putting it off and he called back, only to discover that they didn't want money. They wanted to buy an option that Steve had negotiated to import silk goods from China. Things were looking up. He took the details and promised someone would get back to them.

Then he shut himself away in his office, leaving instructions that he was not to be disturbed. He booted up his computer and inserted the CD holding the files he'd copied from Steve's laptop. And he laid the envelope containing Steve's letter on his blotter.

If Francesca's confession had been in the nature of a hand grenade, the letter had all the allure of an unexploded bomb, and he put it, unopened, to one side. First he had to know how bad things were—and, since Steve had cashed in his life policy, it had to be bad.

He spent the afternoon picking over the financial

bones of Steve's company. It did not make for happy reading.

The business had initially been successful. Supplemented by the money that should have been used as a deposit for the house it had made enough to support the lavish lifestyle Steve had created for himself and Francesca. But in these recessionary days it was making little more than enough to pay his staff and sometimes that had been a close shave. As Guy had suspected, Steven had cashed in his life policy in a desperate bid to reduce his overdraft and hold off the bank. But he hadn't cut back on his own expenses.

And in the last six months, since he'd been sick, it had simply been ticking over with repeat orders. Basically, it was a one-man band. If he wasn't out there finding new stock, drumming up new business...

It could probably be saved, turned around. It would need some painful pruning to reduce costs and someone at the helm who knew what they were doing. Time maybe for Francesca to exercise her marketing muscles. Work for her designer dresses.

As for personal expenses, the lease, property taxes and utilities were the biggest drain and nothing could be done about them. Then there was Connie to pay, the fees for Toby's private nursery school. And keeping Francesca on her pedestal didn't come cheap.

Just as well she was keen to step down.

Finally, when he could put it off no longer, he opened Steve's letter.

It was handwritten and, as he read it, he could hear his brother's voice as clearly as if he was sitting alongside him, saying the words.

Guy, if you're reading this I guess I've cashed in my chips before I've been able to make everything right and, as always, you're the one picking up the pieces. Just as well you've had so much practice.

You already know what I'm asking you to do. You'll know why, too. I want Toby to have two parents. To be loved by someone who knows what I went through and will never allow that to happen to him. Fran may not see it that way but I've left her with nothing. Less than nothing.

We had a good first year, but you know me, I wasn't built for the long haul. I just wish I could have lived up to her. Frankly, it was something of a relief when I opened a letter from a lawyer and discovered that she'd been married before. Just to know that she wasn't perfect, you know? I did tell you it was her decision, but I don't blame you for not believing me… Not that I ever let her know that I'd found out. Read her letters. Besides, my secrets were far worse. The house, the money I owe.

Take care of her, Guy. And my boy. Duty, honour—you're so much better at that stuff than I ever was and so is she. I know she'll do what's right.

I've not been the best of partners, I'll be the first to admit it. But she was always loyal and true. I didn't deserve her and, believe me, I know that the night that condom broke was the luckiest in my entire life.

Okay, this is getting tough, and I want to finish it before she comes back. I've told that wet lawyer to lay the 'wishes of a dying man' bit on thick, but I don't suppose he will. You're going to have to do that for me. Tell her it's for Toby. That should do it. And, if she's still not willing, add in Matty and Connie. Without her they're going to be in real trouble.

About the money, Guy. Well, it's too late for sorry and I'd do it again like a shot given the chance. To be honest, I still can't believe I kidded you so easily. You're usually sharper than that, less trusting. I don't think I'd even have tried if I hadn't seen the way you looked at Fran that night. You're usually so good at hiding your feelings, but when I walked in behind her you were lit up... I can tell you now that it frightened the life out of me because I knew I never deserved someone like her. Let's face it I'm so shallow that I make a puddle look deep, while you... Well, let's just say that I know your worth, even if I never admitted it. I couldn't risk you coming back, though. Finding out. That's why I provoked that final row. You throw a mean punch, brother, but it was worth the pain just to keep you away.

I can't tell you how much I missed you.

Steve

'Idiot,' Guy said, but softly. 'I missed you, too, brother.'

He dropped the letter on his desk and stood up. He needed to think. Needed air.

Leaving his car at the office, he headed in the direction of Green Park, but it was too small to do more than take the edge off his driving need to do what his brother had asked. To move mountains, divert rivers, change the world for Francesca Lang.

That she was in trouble was clear. Whether she knew how much trouble might not yet have dawned on her, but she had no house, no money, no job and a company that, if it was a horse, someone would have taken out and shot.

That she would resent his interference in her life after an absence that she believed was due to his own personal pettiness was crystal clear. She loathed him and, right now, he didn't blame her. He certainly hadn't done anything to improve the situation since he'd arrived.

He could show her the letter. The temptation to be absolved…made whole in her eyes…was almost overwhelming. But that would diminish Steve. And expose his own feelings for her.

She didn't need that. What she needed was to be able to believe that he was going to marry her purely out of duty and guilt. And was going to keep his distance.

Fran poured a couple of glasses of wine from a bottle she'd found open in the fridge and handed one to Matty. 'Today is a day I never want to repeat,' she said, raising her glass. 'Here's to the back of it.'

'That tough?'

'Honestly?' she asked.

'That would probably be best,' Matty replied.

'Well, the good news is that I won't have to sell the house to pay inheritance tax on it.'

'Well, that *is* good. What's the bad news?'

'I won't have to sell it because Steven didn't own it.'

The silence was complex. Full of unspoken thoughts. Fran wished she'd kept that news to herself. At least for the time being. But she needed to talk to somebody…

'I thought you said he bought it from Guy,' Matty finally managed.

'That's what Steven told me. Apparently he was being economical with the truth. The house did once belong to the family, but was sold off by his father some years ago. It was just chance it happened to be available to let when we were looking for somewhere to live.'

Matty choked as she swallowed a mouthful of her drink and let slip an expletive. 'What did Guy have to say about that?'

'It's none of his business, Matty.'

'Look, I don't want to sound over-anxious, but you're going to need someone on your side—'

'Not him,' she snapped back.

'Is there anyone else?'

'You don't understand—'

'I understand the situation perfectly. Guy Dymoke is the devil himself. The one whose name must never be spoken. Anyone would think the pair of you had had a passionate affair or something—'

'No!' Then, because she knew she'd overreacted, 'We only met once before. When Steven and I had dinner with him when we told him that we were moving in together. And about the baby.'

'Oh, please! I wouldn't have blamed you. I thought he was absolutely dishy. I gave the eyelashes a thorough workout but, charming though he was, I could see I was wasting my time. The man was too distracted to notice.'

'Distracted? Who by?' She felt her face grow warm. 'Not that it matters,' she said quickly. 'If he chose to flirt at the funeral reception—'

'Did I say he was flirting?' She didn't answer. 'He was distracted, that's all.'

'Guilt-ridden, more like. Guy and Steven had a difficult relationship and I made it worse. He thought we should have got married and gave Steven a hard time about it. Thought he was the one who wouldn't commit.'

'Oh, I see.'

'At least I could put that right.'

'You told him? About your marriage?'

'I had to.'

'Oh, I see. You wanted *him* to feel guilty.'

'I feel guilty enough for both of us, Matty. But I have no doubt he's wishing he'd taken the time to mend fences.'

'How do you know he didn't? Steven might have had his own reasons for not wanting a family reunion. He probably owed him money.' Fran was too slow with her reassurance. 'He did, didn't he?'

She caught the edge of panic in Matty's voice as it began to dawn on her that her home was now seriously at risk. 'No. No, of course not,' she said reassuringly. 'And I'll have the company up and running at full speed again before you know. I'm looking forward to the challenge. We'll be fine.'

'Good. I like having a roof over my head.'

'I'm really sorry about the money you spent. I know—'

'Don't…' Matty reached out, took her hand. 'Don't blame yourself. I would have done it anyway. Where else would I go, for heaven's sake?'

Don't blame yourself?

That was easier said than done. She'd been sleep-walking through life. If she'd cared enough she'd have known…

'What about the lease? How long is it for? Did the lawyer say anything about that?'

Tom Palmer hadn't said anything much. If she hadn't prompted him she'd still have been in blissful ignorance about the house, and it occurred to her that even now he'd probably kept back more than he'd revealed. She'd seen the silent exchange between Tom Palmer and Guy. The 'we'll talk about this later' look, decide what to do when there isn't a hysterical female to disrupt proceedings. No wonder he'd bustled her out…

But she managed a reassuring smile for Matty. 'There's nothing to worry about. Guy said he'd deal with all the loose ends.'

All she had to do was marry him.

'He can't be that bad, then.'

'What? Oh, I don't know. One minute I'm convinced he loathes me, the next he's being so sweet with Toby…'

'Don't drive him away, Fran. Toby will need a good man to be there for him.'

'The way he was there for Steven?'

'You've only heard Steven's side of that.' She didn't add… *The man who lied to you about this house.* But then she didn't have to. 'He was Steven's brother, Fran. Toby's uncle.' She held out her glass for a refill. 'Besides, he's very ornamental. The kind of man you'd want to share a sofa with on a cold winter's night when there was nothing on the television.'

'It's a little soon to be thinking that way.'

'For you, maybe. Not for me.' Then she laughed. 'It's okay. I promise I'll be good.'

'Don't bother for me,' she managed, but her laugh was too brittle. 'If he whisked you away to a life of luxury and ease that would be enough for me.'

But it would mean seeing them together. Living with it every day...

'Enough for you, maybe. I'd want a man who was around a little more of the time. Besides, there isn't just me,' Matty pointed out. 'There's Toby. And Connie. And that stray cat Steven didn't know you kept fed on the finest cat food.'

'She visits half a dozen houses in this street. I don't think I'm prepared to sacrifice my virtue so that she can eat.'

'No. I'm sorry. That was uncalled for. I guess I'm edgier than I thought.'

'It'll be okay, Matty. I'll talk to Tom Palmer. He'll mediate with the landlord's agent if necessary. There's no reason why they should terminate the lease. I was Steven's partner, after all. I'm sure there's some legal thing about being able to hand a lease on...'

To next of kin. Or a wife. She was neither.

'Okay. But don't leave it too long to sort out the details, will you. As I said, I like to sleep at night. And in the meantime we're going to have to re-negotiate our arrangements. Just paying my expenses isn't good enough any more.'

'This is a nightmare. I can't tell you how sorry I am—'

'Enough. It isn't your fault.' And Matty waved away her apology. 'And I'm beginning to get back on my feet.' She pulled a face. 'Where work is concerned, anyway. So, how did you get on at the office this morning?' she asked, firmly changing the subject.

'I never got there. After visiting the lawyer we came back here.'

'We?'

'Guy and me.' Matty's eyebrows rose a fraction. 'We decided we'd better go through Steven's things first,' she said quickly. 'He copied some files from the laptop…'

'What's so funny?'

'Funny?'

'You were smiling.'

Fran curbed a smile that had somehow sneaked beneath her defences and said, 'Oh, nothing. He let Toby think he was helping, that's all. Then he took them home to study while I went through Steven's briefcase.' This time Matty's eyebrows shot up. 'He's Steven's executor. Not that there's much to execute.'

She groaned inwardly at the apparent callousness of her remark.

'It's me, Fran. You don't have to pretend.'

'No. No more pretence.' Then, 'But I wrote a pile of cheques last week for bills, including Toby's nursery fees. I'm going to need to know if the bank will honour them. They may be a little less relaxed about the overdraft now that Steven is dead.'

'I suggest you leave the bank to fight that one out with the lawyers.'

'No, Matty. I've been living in a dream world. Letting life happen to me instead of taking it by the scruff of the neck and taking control.' She looked up at the ceiling. 'We have a lease, but I suspect it's one on a house of cards, one that's going to collapse around my ears unless I do something to stop it.'

Matty made no attempt to reassure her, which was worrying. Instead she said, 'What did you have in mind?' Then, 'Have you got *anything* in mind?'

'Actually, I've got a three point plan. One,' she said, ticking them off on her fingers, 'I'm going into the bank on Monday to see exactly where I stand. Reduce any outgoings that aren't absolutely essential.' She managed a grin. 'I'm not going to have time to waste at the health club for a start. From now on I'll have to take the cheap keep-fit option and run in the park.'

'Whatever turns you on.'

'Then I'm going to have to find out what Steven was planning when he was taken ill. He had something in mind, but said it would wait until he was feeling better.' She hadn't pushed him. Hadn't wanted him to see that she knew he was never going to get well, although obviously he'd eventually worked it out for himself. 'I've been going through his stuff trying to find out what it was, but all I can find is some paperwork written in Chinese.'

'Why don't you try the local Chinese takeaway? Someone there might be able to help.' Then, 'Sorry. I don't suppose sarcasm helps. What's number three?'

'Hot and sour soup, isn't it?'

Matty pulled a face. 'I meant on the three point plan.'

Marry Guy Dymoke.

She pulled herself together. 'I'm going to buy a Lottery ticket.'

CHAPTER FIVE

EASY enough to announce that she was answering the wake-up call that fate had rung so loudly in her ears. It was quite another to look the world in the eye at eight o'clock in the morning—and most of it appeared to be packed into the underground train with her—and act on it.

Francesca had put in a couple of years at the coal face of marketing before she'd met Steven. It hadn't exactly been a riveting experience. What ideas she'd offered had been brushed aside before, as the most junior member of the team, she'd been despatched for coffee, sandwiches, photocopying. She hadn't needed too much persuading not to return after Toby was born. None of the wives or partners of Steven's business friends had worked, and it had been easy enough to fall into the round of gym workouts, lunches and dinner parties. To pretend to herself that she had a full and rewarding life.

Easy to pretend that she was happy. Bury the memory of a moment when the world had appeared to light up. Steven was Toby's father. They were a family and she would never do anything that would tear them apart. Even if some days she had felt as if she was being crushed by cotton wool...

No more. From now on she was going to keep both feet firmly on the ground. Make a new start. And as she stepped out of the station and into the daylight she tugged her jacket firmly into place. At least she looked the part. But then that was easy. She'd been playing the role of perfect partner, mother and hostess for so long that she could do it with her eyes closed.

But this wasn't playing house. Make believe happy families. This was the real world and she wasn't fooling herself into believing that the right suit and a confident smile was going to be enough. But it was a start.

Thankfully she wouldn't have to confront the staff immediately. She'd have an hour before anyone arrived. An hour to sort through Steven's desk and root out any more little bombshells he'd kept hidden from her. An hour to fit herself behind his desk and make it look as if she belonged there and maybe come up with a plan to fill the big empty space in her brain. If not, she thought as she unlocked the door and let herself into the small, rather scruffy office and storage area tucked away in a courtyard beside the canal, it would be a question of playing it by ear...

Easing the key from the lock she heard a drawer being opened in the little cubby hole that served Steven as his private office.

Had she walked in on a break-in?

A muttered curse released her. She'd know that voice anywhere, and just at that moment a burglar would have been more welcome, but she closed the door quietly and crossed the outer office.

Guy looked as if he'd been there all night. Dishevelled, unshaven, gaunt with fatigue and almost unbearably desirable. She'd coped with the first shock of seeing him at the funeral because, numb with the tragedy that had overtaken her and Toby, she had somehow been immune. Functioning on automatic. Beyond any real feeling. But his arrival had jolted her out of her emotional stasis and each unexpected appearance battered at her defences. Anger helped shore them up, but seeing him like this utterly demolished them. Just like the first time when she'd walked into that restaurant and lost her heart.

When it had already been too late.

She'd told herself that it was nonsense. That her hormones were in turmoil. That Steven was the father of her child. That he was kind and funny and charming and she'd have married him like a shot if it had been possible, just as Guy had urged.

Right at the moment she yearned to go to him, put her arms around him and comfort him, as he'd comforted her yesterday when she'd practically thrown herself into his arms. When he'd backed off as quickly as decency allowed, she reminded herself.

No. She'd keep all thoughts of comfort to herself. He despised her enough already without any suggestion that, in deep financial trouble, she was ready to throw herself at the nearest man with a fat wallet. Particularly not one she'd berated for his lack of feeling.

'What's the matter, Guy?' she said, as he slammed the drawer shut. 'Couldn't you find what you were looking for?'

At least she had the doubtful satisfaction of seeing him completely thrown for once. He hadn't heard her let herself in and he visibly started as he looked up and saw her standing in the doorway. Had the grace to look uncomfortable at being caught with his hands in Steven's desk.

'Steve wasn't the greatest record keeper. I suspect that it was deliberate. That he didn't want to know how far out on a limb he was.' Then, 'What time is it?' he asked, raking his fingers through his hair before dragging his hands over his face.

'Just after eight,' she told him, trying not to worry too much about the 'out on a limb' remark. 'Would you care to explain how you got in?'

Even as she said it, she saw the bunch of keys lying on the desk. She reached out and picked them up before he realised what she was going to do. Beating him to them by a heartbeat. But then he did look as if he hadn't slept all night.

She held them up, letting them dangle from her finger, looking at them as if they were a strange and foreign object. 'Where did you get these? Did Tom Palmer give them to you? I thought the company belonged to me now.'

'It does,' he replied wearily. 'Tom didn't give them to me.'

She waited, but since he didn't enlighten her she said, 'So? Did you help yourself to them from Steven's briefcase? Take a unilateral decision not to disturb the little lady's dusty brain cells? Expect her to be able to think for herself...'

'No. You don't—'

'What? Understand?'

This time he didn't even bother to try to explain.

'What, Guy? Are you telling me it's worse than that? How could it be any worse?' On second thoughts, that wasn't such a stretch either. 'Don't tell me Steven didn't own this place, either?' And, when he didn't answer, 'Oh, great. Were you underwriting his business too?'

'No. I helped him with the lease when he needed somewhere. Just to get him started.'

'So it was all talk? Not just the house, but the business too? Steven was a man of straw and you were his prop and mainstay. Why did you walk away from him?'

'He didn't need me any more, Francesca. Married or not, he had you and he didn't need me around. I told you.'

'Yes, you told me. But what about him? How did he feel about that?'

'Oh, rest assured, he was completely happy about it.'

That stopped her. She didn't ask why. Didn't want to believe that Steven had seen that split second reaction, that moment when she'd first set eyes on Guy Dymoke and seen a different future. An impossible future...

A bit wobbly around the knees, she sank on to the secretary's chair placed at an angle to the desk and for a moment or two all she could hear was the sound of her own heartbeat hammering in her ears. The silence gathering.

After what seemed like for ever, Guy finally said, 'Is that it? Have you finished?'

'What?' She shook her head. 'I'm sorry. I interrupted you. You were telling me about the keys.'

'Brian Hicks called me yesterday, asked me to come down and see him at the office.'

Steven's office manager? 'How did he know your number? Why didn't he phone me?' Then, 'Why didn't you?'

'It was late.'

'I'm allowed out after dark, Guy. I mean, it's not as if I'm a proper widow or anything—'

'I thought you'd want to be with Toby,' he said,

cutting off her sarcasm. 'I was going to talk to you this morning.'

'It's morning. I'm here. Talk to me.'

'I met him at the reception. After the funeral. He seemed anxious about something so I gave him my card and told him to ring me if he needed any urgent decisions made.'

'How cosy. Clearly it didn't occur to either of you that I might actually want to be bothered. To know what was going on.'

'It wasn't like that. He didn't know what to do. He assumed you'd need some time to—'

'To what? Grieve? I mourned Steven as I watched him die. All I can feel now is relief that he isn't suffering any more. Now I have to think of Toby and Matty and Connie and the people who work here. All the people who are relying on me.'

'Well, you don't have to worry about Mr Hicks. He gave me his keys and this.' He pushed an envelope towards her. 'It's his resignation. He asked me to tell you that he's sorry, but he's found another job.'

Shocked, she said, 'So soon?'

'He'd apparently been looking for some time.'

It was just as well she was sitting down. 'Would it be paranoid of me to suggest that the words "sinking ship" seem appropriate at this point? Not that I'm suggesting Brian is a rat.' She realised that he was looking at her with concern and she straightened her back, forced herself to meet his gaze head on. 'He has a family to consider. Did he say anything else?'

'Apparently a couple of the staff were temps. He let them go last month. You appear to be left with Steven's secretary—that would be the young woman in tears at the reception—?'

'Claire. Yes, she was very upset. The poor girl had a terrible crush on Steven. She wasn't his type and I told him off once for flirting with her. That it wasn't kind…' Then, realising that she'd implied a lot more than she'd said, she quickly went on, 'He said it saved him paying her what she was actually worth.'

Which, if possible, sounded even worse, and she bit her lip. Concentrated all her attention on the keys that were cutting into her palm she was holding on to them so tightly.

'Brian Hicks,' she said, coming back to the point. 'He must be owed money. Salary, holiday entitlement. Until I've been to the bank…'

'I paid him.'

'Oh. Well, thank you. I'll reimburse you, of course,' she said, mentally crossing her fingers. She had no idea what the company finances were like.

'It's not necessary. We're going to be partners, remember.'

'No.' She didn't want Guy's disturbing presence invading her life. Him being there every time she turned around. She'd had three years of feeling guilty because every time she closed her eyes…

'It's what Steve wanted. The dying wish of a man who loved you,' he said. 'It will make everything simpler, although I do intend to be a silent partner. In all aspects of the arrangement,' he added.

'You mean you don't anticipate leaping into my bed with the same speed with which you've taken over my office?'

'I somehow doubt that's what Steve had in mind. I don't suppose he imagined that you'd feel like leaping into anyone's bed for some time.'

'No. I'm sorry. You're the one who's been lumbered with all of us. You should be getting angry, not me.'

'I think you've got reason enough to be more than a touch irritated. I, at least, have gained a family.' She looked up, surprised by something unexpected in his voice. A warmth... He was looking down at the notepad in front of him. 'It would seem your staff now consists of Claire and a young lad who appears to be on some kind of work scheme.'

'Jason,' she said and, since he was keeping it businesslike, she did the same. 'That will certainly cut the overheads.' Then, 'Tell me, in your search through Steven's office, did you come across any good news?'

'Not much. I went through everything with Brian before he left. The company is still just about ticking over on repeat orders. You need new stock, though. And to take less money out the business for it to prosper and grow. I've laid it all out for you,' he said, indicating the notepad, then sitting back in the big chair, seeming to fill it in a way that Steven never had. 'One of the problems is that the company seems to have had no real focus. Steve imported anything that caught his eye and, to be honest, he didn't always get it right. Too many times he's had to sell on at a loss just to shift the goods. I suspect the bank will be disinclined to continue extending the overdraft in the present circumstances.'

'Then I'll have to convince them otherwise. Quickly.'

'The sooner we tie up the loose ends, the better.'

She didn't ask what 'loose ends' he was referring to. Just said, 'Is there any more bad news?'

'Well, there's the lease on this place.'

Fran belatedly wished she hadn't been quite so sarcastic about the lease. One look at his face made her wish that Guy did own it.

'What about the lease?'

'It expires in two months' time. The rent increase being asked is going to be a problem unless business picks up quickly.'

She couldn't think of any response that would adequately convey the way she felt, so she said, 'Not much good news, you said. That implies there is some.'

'That depends on your point of view. You've got a store room filled with stock. Most of it has been there for years, by the look of it. It'll give you something to practice your marketing skills on.'

'You're not going to stay around and help with that, too?'

'That's your line of expertise, Francesca. I have to get back to my own business. In fact, I'm grateful you tore up the tickets to St Lucia. A trip to the local register office will be far more convenient.'

'Well, thanks. I needed that bit of good news. No house. No company premises. Just a load of old stock that Steven couldn't sell and a cheap ten-minute wedding to keep the bank happy.'

'Low-key was what I had in mind. I don't imagine it will prove to be cheap,' he replied. 'Of course, if you'd like to throw a party to celebrate the occasion I'm sure Connie can manage a few of her more exciting sandwiches.'

She flushed. 'There isn't going to be a wedding. Low-key or otherwise. I will not marry you just to keep a roof over my head!'

'No, you'll marry me to provide Toby with a roof over his head in accordance with his father's dying wishes. Not forgetting your cousin and Mrs Constantinopoulos.'

'You took the trouble to find out her name?'

'I needed it for my company payroll. In the meantime you might get Jason to start on an inventory of stock so that you can sell it before it gets seized by creditors.'

You?

Her.

He really was going to leave her to run it?

'Is there anything else?'

'Yes. Those characters who were hassling you at the funeral. They weren't after money. Apparently, Steve managed to persuade some Chinese co-operative into giving him sole rights to import all their goods for a year. Something to do with silk, I think. They've been buying it from him, but now that...' He checked himself. 'They represent another importing company who are prepared to pay you a substantial sum of money to take over the remainder of the option. I've been looking for it.'

'Oh. Well, there was something in his briefcase that might have been it. It was written in Chinese characters. With a little chop mark. I thought I should get it translated.'

'The sooner the better. Find out exactly what it's worth before you part with it.'

Silk. She liked the sound of that...

Then, realising that she was still clutching the spare set of office keys, she dropped them into her bag. 'You look exhausted, Guy. How long have you been here?'

'Too long, but my body clock is shot to hell.'

'You're fortunate that it's just your body clock

that's gone wrong,' she said sharply, her apparent lack of sympathy a desperate bid to ignore something in his voice that tugged at the very core of her being. Being angry was the only way to keep her feelings at bay.

His expression didn't change but she could feel his reaction: it was almost physical, as if he'd been slapped.

'In comparison with what happened to Steve, your own problems, it was tactless to even mention it.'

'No!' Immediately full of remorse she said, 'I'm sorry, Guy. I'm not the only one who's lost someone. I'm just…' She didn't know what she was feeling. A bit lost. Very confused. But mostly just empty, when everyone expected her to be racked with grief. It was as if her emotional core had been injected with Novocain and was completely numb. And, since the funeral, there had been so much else to worry about. 'You should get some sleep,' she said.

'What about you? How are you managing?'

'Keeping busy helps.'

'Sufficiently to counteract the threat of bankruptcy, the risk of losing your home?'

She reached out, put her hand over his. 'Go home, Guy.'

'Home?' He withdrew his hand, pinched the bridge of his nose between his fingers as if to stave off the tiredness. 'I don't have a home. I just have a barn of an apartment that I bought as an investment. Every luxury. No…warmth.' Then, 'I don't suppose you'd consider having breakfast with me?'

'At your luxurious but cold apartment?' She forced a smile. 'Are you sure you don't mean will I cook it for you?'

'I mean, will you come and have breakfast with me? As in, can I buy you breakfast? There must be somewhere nearby that can rustle up half a pint of espresso and a bacon sandwich two inches thick. For once in my life I can't face the thought of eating alone.'

She put the temptation to take him up on the invitation firmly behind her. 'The last thing you need is espresso—' the last thing he needed was to go home to an empty apartment '—and I really need to stay here and go through a few things before everyone arrives. But there's no reason for you to be alone. Go to Elton Street. If Connie's on your payroll I don't see why she shouldn't make you a bacon sandwich. As thick as you like. She can speak English, more or less, but she can't read it very well. Did Matty tell you about her?'

'She just suggested that the sandwiches might be a risk, although it's hard to imagine how she could mess up on something that simple.'

'For heaven's sake, it was just once. Anyone can make a mistake—' She stopped. He didn't want to hear about her domestic arrangements.

'Where did you find her?'

Apparently he did.

'In the park, if you must know. I'd seen her feeding the ducks there. Talked to her. She's Greek. Came here years ago to marry some café owner who used her as free labour until he left her with a mountain of bills she couldn't pay and, terrified by debt collectors, she just packed what she could carry and ran away. She just spiralled downwards until she ended up in a hostel for the homeless. I knew I ought to do something about her but I didn't know what. Then one day

she just keeled over in front of me and I realised that
I had known what to do all along. I'd just been putting
it off.'

'You took her home?'

She could understand his astonishment. 'Once bit-
ten?' she replied. 'This was different, Guy.'

'Yes. Of course it was. How did Steve take it?'

'He understood that I couldn't send her back to that
horrible place,' she said crisply, not wanting to remember how hard he'd tried to talk her into doing
just that. How angry he'd been that she'd even been
talking to some bag lady. Even angrier at her letting
Toby talk to her. How irritated he'd been to discover
that his 'princess' had a stubborn streak. They'd almost had a row. She'd almost felt alive. But then
Matty had rather slyly pointed out that it was the kind
of thing 'princesses' did... 'All she needed was a
home. To feel useful.'

'That's all?' he said wryly.

'Actually, she was—is—a huge help to Matty, and
she's wonderful with Toby. Look, I really think you
should go home before your body decides it's had
enough and you bang your head on the desk as it
shuts down.'

'I'm touched by your concern.'

'Bag ladies, stray dogs, jet-lagged males, they're
all the same to me. I'm a walking care centre.'

'You have a rescue dog too? I seem to have missed
that one.'

'No. At least not for long. Steven came out in a
rash. He said he was allergic. It was a spaniel.' Damn!
The bloody tears would catch her out... She might
not have been in love with him, but she had loved
him. She couldn't have lived with him otherwise. And

he was Toby's father. 'Anyway, that's not my concern,' she said briskly, refusing to give in to them. 'What's worrying me is that if you fall asleep in that chair I won't be able to get into the desk. Did you come in your car?'

'No, I left it at my office yesterday.'

'Good. You're in no fit state to be behind the wheel.' She dug around in her bag for her front door key—which she laid on the desk in front of him— and a tissue, which she used to blow her nose. And wondered how much of his car Steven had owned. Whether she'd be able to use the money to ease finances a little. It was a company car so it would be hers. The papers must be here...

'Should you be here at all?' he asked, distracting her as he got up, came around the desk. 'This would be tough for anyone.'

His eyes were full of compassion, concern, and something else that she thought might be despair but was more likely exhaustion. She wanted to lay her hand against his cheek. To kiss his brow. To wrap her arms around him and hold him for a moment.

Instead she said, 'Of course I'll cope.' Then she looked at the tissue as if she'd just realised he thought she was crying. 'Oh, this! This is just hay fever.'

'Sure,' he said, not bothering to hide his disbelief.

'Really. It's the autumn kind. Brought on by chrysanthemums. It's quite common, apparently.' But she couldn't quite meet his gaze as she said it. Instead she picked up the key and, taking his hand, she placed it in his palm. 'Take a taxi, let yourself in. Connie will show you where you can crash out, and she'll make you your bacon sandwich while you take a shower. Help yourself to Steven's stuff if you want to shave,' she said, then added, 'Actually, you might be wiser to leave that until after you've slept. We can talk about the business later.'

He closed his fingers around the key, removing his hand from hers as he straightened so that he was towering over her.

'The will is my sole concern. The business is yours.' Then, 'Just don't do anything…' He stopped, obviously thinking better of what he'd been going to say.

'Stupid?'

'You might think I was going to say that but you're going to have to torture me before I'll admit it. You're right. I definitely need to get some sleep. I'll see you later, Francesca.'

As the outer door banged shut behind him, she flinched. What on earth was she doing, feeling sorry for him? He didn't need her compassion. He didn't need anything. He was Guy Dymoke.

Guy made it to Elton Street without falling asleep in the cab. That was because he was too busy storing up those moments when Francesca had reached out, touched his hand. As if she actually cared about him. But he had no illusions. She'd adored Steve and the only reason she'd consider marrying him was because he'd seen it as the only way to provide security for her and her army of dependants.

That's why he'd forced himself to break contact first. Before she became embarrassed by a simple gesture of kindness. Might think he'd mistake it for a gesture of intimacy.

Connie was out but it didn't matter. Breakfast had only been a pretence to stay with her. He was long past food and, realising that a shower would only wake him up, he went straight upstairs to the guest room and ran a bath. He needed to think about the best way to deal with the mess fate—and Steve—had thrown in his lap.

Clever Steve. He had known him so well. Known he'd look after his family come what may. But suggesting a marriage of convenience had meant he would now never be able to show his feelings for Francesca.

He'd marry her because it would be his joy, his honour, his dearest wish. But he could never tell her that.

She'd think he was saying it to make it easy for her. He'd never know if she was accepting him because she had no choice. Out of desperation.

Fran looked at the figures Guy had spent the night putting together for her. He was right. It wasn't good, as he'd no doubt tell her again, in words of one syllable, over dinner.

No. Not dinner. Dinner suggested intimacy.

She'd give him nursery tea in the kitchen with Toby. And she smiled again as she remembered how good he'd been with her little boy. Became solemn again as she remembered Matty's conviction that Toby would need him. Steven hadn't been the best partner in the world, but he had been a good father. The truth was that he'd still been a little boy at heart himself, with that same see-it, want-it irresponsibility.

She dragged her mind back to the job in hand. The company was hers now and, if Guy would give her a little breathing space, she would make a success of it. She took off her jacket, found a brown warehouseman's coat to protect herself against the inevitable dust and switched on the lights in the small warehouse.

She'd heard Steven say often enough that the whole premise of importing fancy goods was to shift them as quickly as possible. Sell before you had to pay. Before the public lost its taste for the latest fad. The unforgiving strip lights immediately revealed why the company was in trouble.

She heard the door bang as someone arrived. 'Claire? Jason?'

Jason appeared in the doorway. 'Hello, Mrs...Miss...'

'Miss Lang, Jason. But please just call me Fran.'

'Oh, right. We weren't expecting you.'

'Unfortunately Brian Hicks has left and so have the temps. It's just you, me—' the door banged again '—and Claire,' she said with considerable relief. 'So, we're going to have to do the best we can between us.' She indicated the cartons that stretched into the darker recesses of the storage room. Calling it a warehouse was an exaggeration even in estate agent terms. 'Have you any idea what all this stuff is?'

He shook his head. 'It was all here when I started.'

She took a deep breath. 'Okay. What I want you to do is make an inventory of all the stock and put a sample of each item on my desk.'

'Everything?'

'Yes, Jason. Everything. Along with a note of how much of each item we have.'

'You want me to count them all?' he asked, without bothering to disguise his lack of enthusiasm.

'Not individually,' she said, curbing her impatience. 'The contents will be on the outside of the boxes.' It would have to be done anyway, so that it could be valued for probate. The sooner the better.

'Shall I put the kettle on first?' he asked. 'Steve usually—'

'No. I want you to get started on the boxes. I'll bring you some coffee.' Later. 'In the meantime will you look out for anything made from silk? From China?'

'Two sugars,' he said.

She was cheerfully brisk with the still red-eyed Claire, asking her if she knew where to find the documents for the car. And when she'd found them she set her searching for the paperwork to match the stock, so that she'd have some idea of how much everything had cost. She could have left it to the valuation consultant but since she didn't know what else to do it gave her the impression she was doing something useful.

Steven's nearly new car, she discovered, was, like everything else, leased rather than owned. She called the company and arranged with them to pick it up. It would be cheaper to take taxis everywhere. And a heck of a lot cheaper to go by bus.

'What shall I say?' Claire asked. 'When people ring and want to know what's happening?'

She didn't know. There was an awful lot she didn't know, she realised. 'Leave a message on the answering machine saying that the office is closed until Monday due to a bereavement.' That would give her breathing space. Time to think. Then, 'Have there been many calls?'

'Dozens. They're all in the day book.'

'I'll take it home with me.'

Then, after glancing at the odd assortment of ob-

jects that Jason was laying out on her desk—paper
fans, pottery frogs that no one but a mother could
love, some particularly hideous lamps—she packed
up all the stuff that Guy had left for her and, leaving
them to get on with the inventory, took the public
transport alternative home. It was cheap but endless,
and she was anxious to get back to the house and take
another look at that Chinese document. Get it translated.

Although, if the rest of the stock was anything to
go by, it wasn't going to be anything to get excited
about.

She dumped her bag in the hall and ran upstairs,
stripping off her jacket, unzipping her skirt as she
went, eager to get on. She'd have to rethink her working wardrobe, she realised. Dark suits and silk shirts
were out for the time being. She didn't have to impress Jason and Claire, and she'd be much more useful wearing the kind of clothes in which she could
help shift and unpack boxes.

She stepped out of her skirt and tossed it on the
bed with her jacket and slipped the buttons on her
shirt. Then, pulling a face at the state of the cuffs
after just a few hours, she crossed to the bathroom to
dump it into the laundry bin.

At which point Chinese characters became the very
last thing on her mind.

CHAPTER SIX

FRANCESCA'S heart stopped. Guy had fallen asleep in the bath. His arm was hanging over the edge, his fingers brushing against the floor. The tension had flowed out of his face and his long, elegant limbs were totally relaxed and, for the first time since he'd come home, she caught a glimpse of the man who had looked at her across a crowded restaurant bar and made her feel as if she was the only woman in the world.

Her gaze drifted down the length of his body, then stopped, transfixed momentarily on what might just have been the movement of water caused by his breathing, or a stirring of something much more dangerous. Her heart kicked back in, racing to catch up as she forced herself to return to his face, certain that he'd be watching her, his eyes mocking…

But no, he was still fast asleep. He looked so much younger, so much more approachable with the harsh lines smoothed from his face. So much more vulnerable…

She really should wake him. If he'd come home and got straight into the bath—although why he was in her bath was a mystery—the water would be cold, but she could scarcely reach out and touch him on his tanned, broad shoulder or stroke back the hair clinging damply to his forehead…

She swallowed.

What she had to do was back out of the bathroom

right now. Very quietly collect her clothes and, once dressed and safely downstairs, she could bang a door or shout to see if Connie was about and leave it to him whether he decided to climb into bed—and presumably that would be her bed, too—or come downstairs.

Guy's first thought was that he must be dreaming. Nothing new there. He dreamed of her all the time, but never before when he'd been lying naked in the bath, with Francesca, clad only in a bra that would stop traffic and a thong that left him in no doubt that the money she spent on bikini waxing was well spent, standing near enough to touch.

Never had it been this real.

His second thought was that if this was a dream, why would the water be cold? That really wasn't fair...

Even so, it was taking every ounce of willpower to remain perfectly still, keep up the pretence that he was asleep so that she could gather her wits and retreat in good order. That way they could both pretend this had never happened. Preferably before the water began to heat back up...

She took a step back, her gaze fixed on his face, ensuring that he did not open his eyes...

Then, very carefully, she took another one. And caught her elbow an eye-watering blow on the edge of the door. At which point there was no need for further pretence.

'It's usually wiser to look where you're going,' he said.

'Is that right?' she snapped. 'Well, thanks. I'll be

sure to remember that for the next occasion I find a man in my bath.'

'I was simply trying to be helpful.'

He wanted to be more than helpful. He wanted to go to her and put his arms around her and kiss the pain away. Hold her so that she would forget everything. Know only him.

He doubted that she'd appreciate the thought, let alone the gesture. Besides, she was clutching her left elbow with her right hand and was bent almost double, a position which was doing indescribable things to her cleavage which, cold water notwithstanding, left him in a position where concealment was the only option.

'You were just pretending to be asleep, weren't you?' she demanded, glaring at him.

He thought of denying it. Decided against it.

'I thought it might save us both considerable embarrassment,' he said somewhat thickly as he attempted to summon up a memory of the months he'd once spent in the Antarctic. *Cold. Freezing cold. Frostbite cold...* 'I have to admit, I didn't expect you to take quite so long over your retreat.'

'I was just...' she forgot about her elbow long enough to make a vague gesture as she sought some kind of explanation '...taken by surprise. That's all.'

'So was I, but in my case it was excusable.'

'Excuse me? I offered you the guest room.'

'And?'

'Which is at the end of the hall,' she cut in. 'With its own small, but perfectly adequate bathroom.' Then, 'Why didn't you lock the door?'

'It never occurred to me. In the field there isn't a door. At home there isn't anyone to keep out.'

Struggling to maintain his composure in the face of extreme provocation he said, 'Look, would you pass me a towel?'

'Get it yourself!'

'Fair enough.' He'd tried. A man could only do so much... But as he sat up, water cascading from him, she latched on to the flaw in that arrangement and said, 'No, wait! I'll do it.' And she pulled a towel down from a stack on the shelf and passed it to him, looking pointedly the other way as he stood up, wrapped it firmly about his waist and stepped out of the tub.

'I still don't understand why you're in here,' she said, not letting the matter drop. The fact that she was wearing next to nothing herself had obviously slipped her mind. 'Connie wouldn't have put you in my room. And why didn't you leave your clothes all over the floor to warn me that you were here, like any normal man?'

'Because I hung them up.' He reached over her head and unhooked his clothes from the back of the door.

'You're housetrained?'

'Don't bank on it,' he said. Right at that moment, the civilised veneer of the modern man was being strained to breaking point and he was using the armful of clothes to disguise the fact. 'But I have lived in some places where clothes left lying on the floor are an open invitation to the kind of creatures you wouldn't want to share with. It gets to be a habit.'

'You'll make some woman a great husband,' she said. Then clearly wished she'd kept her mouth shut.

'I believe it takes rather more than the ability to hang up your own clothes. Being in the same country for at least fifty per cent of the time would seem to be fairly high up on the list.'

'I know a lot of women who'd be delighted with that arrangement.'

'Is that right? Then since I don't usually manage to spend more than ten per cent of my time in London you'll be the envy of your friends, won't you?'

'You don't think I'm actually going to tell anyone?' Then quickly, 'Even if I was prepared to contemplate marrying you.'

'You've married for someone else's convenience. I don't see why you'd find it so difficult to marry for your own.' Then, realising that probably wasn't the best way to convince her, he said, 'Look, I'm sorry for intruding on your space, but Connie wasn't in when I arrived and since this was the guest room the last time I stayed here I assumed it still was. Don't you use the master suite?'

'No—' Then, 'Well, yes. Of course. But—'

But it had been Steve's sickroom. She'd nursed him in there. She probably never wanted to go into that room again.

'I'm sorry. That was incredibly stupid of me. Obviously you wouldn't want to sleep in there.'

'No...' Her mouth made the shape, but no sound emerged. She cleared her throat. 'No.'

'Maybe I could have it redecorated for you? When you're ready. If that would help.'

'What's the point? It's just temporary. I'll be looking for somewhere else just as soon as I've got the business sorted out.'

He wanted to tell her to stop being so stupid. He wanted to take her by the shoulders and shake her and tell her that he'd move heaven and earth to keep her safe in the home she loved. His body was way ahead of his mind and he made a move towards the door, needing to put an end to this torture. She still didn't move.

'I imagine that's where I'll find a razor, then?' he prompted, not prepared to get any closer. There was altogether too much naked flesh in a confined space to risk that. 'Across the hall?'

She frowned, as if coming back from somewhere inside her head. 'Oh, yes. And Steven's clothes. Please do help yourself to whatever you like…'

And that was when she realised that she was somewhat underdressed to offer that kind of invitation. Underdressed full stop. And blushed all the way down to her toes.

'A clean shirt. Socks,' she rushed on. 'There's a new toothbrush in the cupboard under…'

'Thank you. I'll find it.'

'Right, I'll go and, um…' She made a vague gesture at her figure, indicating that she was going to put some clothes on, changed her mind about drawing further attention to herself halfway through and, practically falling over her feet, made a rapid retreat, this time face forward to avoid further disaster.

As he waited, giving her time to clear the room, he realised he should have asked her how her elbow was doing. Unfortunately, the quick flash of her smooth, golden backside as she'd finally turned and fled had knocked it clean out of his mind.

Francesca didn't hang around to ask whether Guy was going to continue his nap or would prefer to go downstairs and have something to eat. She just grabbed the first clothes that came to hand and bolted. And, having gathered up the paperwork she'd brought back from the office, she shut herself away in the study.

Her jeans were the comfortable baggy fit cut that she'd worn when Steven wasn't around to grumble that she looked untidy, the top something loose and equally figure obscuring. It felt disloyal somehow— even in the last couple of weeks, when he'd hardly been able to lift his head, he'd still wanted to see her looking like his 'princess'—but it was too late to think about changing. Too late to think about obscuring anything, too.

Guy had seen everything there was to see while she'd stood there talking to him as if they were at a cocktail party, instead of quietly retreating the minute she'd realised that the bathroom was occupied.

In retrospect it was so obvious that she should have simply turned around and walked out. She couldn't imagine what had possessed her to just stand there, gawping like a complete idiot. Or maybe she could, she just didn't want to think about it too hard. Maybe she should stop thinking about it now.

She definitely shouldn't be thinking about that moment when she'd seen the flash of anger burn in his eyes, the involuntary movement of his hand when she'd rejected his offer to redecorate the master bedroom. As if it was something he needed to do to make up for his blunder over mentioning it.

In fact her best plan would be to go out, she decided. Right now. And, grabbing Steven's briefcase— she'd put everything back in so the Chinese stuff had to be in there—she checked the landing to ensure that the way was clear and then went quietly downstairs to find Connie and tell her about their guest.

Toby was having his lunch, and she gave him a big

hug, admired the pictures he'd made at nursery school, had a tiny bite of the fish finger he offered her and let herself out through the back door to avoid the risk of running into Guy in the hall. She needed a little time to eradicate the image of him lying in the bath, the embarrassment of her berating him in her underwear, before she could face him again.

As she walked towards the gate, she saw Matty working at her drawing board, undoubtedly catching up with work put on hold while she'd spent time with her.

Another thing to feel guilty about, she thought as she walked down the road towards the market.

When she returned, it was Guy she wanted to talk to.

'He go,' Connie said. 'I want to make him something nice for lunch, like you say, but he see fish fingers and he eat them with Toby.'

'Good grief. Weren't they cold?'

Connie waggled her hand to suggest they had been neither hot nor cold. 'He say is okay. He make himself sandwich.'

Guy Dymoke had eaten fish finger sandwiches for his lunch? She decided she didn't want to go there. It made him seem much too human. As if she needed proof…

'When…' She cleared her throat. 'When did he leave?'

'Not long. He stay and talk with Toby until nap time, then he go. He have things to do. He say you not to worry. He take care of everything.'

That was more like it. Managing, bossy… Somewhere else.

'That's it?'

'He went to see Matty. Maybe he tell her where he go. Maybe he still there?'

Matty? Something very like jealousy caught in her throat as she remembered how easily the two of them had talked. How he'd smiled at her cousin when he never smiled at her. How Matty had thought him very fanciable…

She caught herself. That was vile. How could she be jealous of her cousin? She should be glad…

She *was* glad. She was just disappointed that Guy wasn't there, that was all. He'd said she'd been offered a substantial sum to surrender the sole importation rights. She wanted to know how much. Wanted his advice. Because if it was valuable enough for someone to want to pay good money for it as a matter of urgency…

On the other hand, maybe it was just as well Guy had gone home. She was already beginning to rely on him. He'd made it clear that the company was her concern and she had to start thinking things through for herself. Besides, there were more pressing concerns. If she wasn't going to marry him she needed to talk to the landlord's agents. Negotiate a new lease for the house.

Apparently using nothing but thin air.

The sooner, the better.

'Right. Well, I'm going to the study.'

Connie placed her hands on her hips. 'And when are you going to eat? Tell me that.'

She'd been saying the same thing every day for weeks. Today she had an answer. 'I had a bowl of soup while I was out.'

'Ha! My soup not good enough for you?'

'It was a business lunch, Connie.'

She'd been given a bowl of chicken soup by the owner of the local Chinese restaurant while his teenage son translated the document she'd found. Steven had been very fond of Chinese food and they'd all been so sweet to her. So kind. She'd even managed a couple of mouthfuls of the soup.

Connie wasn't impressed by her 'business lunch', however. 'What kind of business you do dressed like that, huh? What would Mr Steven say if he saw you go out like that?'

'Steven isn't with us any more, Connie. I have to do things my way from now on.' And it was about time she made a start. 'I'll be upstairs if you need me.'

She phoned Claire to check how things were going.

'The inventory is complete and I've found most of the paperwork.'

'Okay, leave it on the desk and lock up. I'll see you both on Monday.'

'You're going to carry on?'

'That's the plan.' Then, 'Claire, tell me about the silk goods that Steven's been importing. I didn't see anything among the stuff Jason was unpacking.'

'No, the shipments went straight out the moment they arrived. The perfect deal, Steve said.'

'Haven't you got any samples? A catalogue.'

'Not a catalogue.'

'But surely he must have had something to show buyers?'

'Well, there were a few bits and pieces,' she admitted.

'And where are they now? Claire?'

'When Steven didn't... When the company... I thought it was a crime to just let them lie there in a cupboard gathering dust. And it doesn't matter does it? I mean they were a guaranteed sale. You didn't need samples—'

'Are you saying that you took them?' Then, quickly, 'Look, I don't mind. I just need to have a look at whatever you've got.'

'Well, I gave one of the wrappers to my mother, but I've got the other one. I suppose you want it back?'

'No, Claire. You can keep it, but I really need to see it. I want you to go home now and bring it to the house.'

'Now? But that will take for ever and I've got a—'

'Claire!'

'I'll be as quick as I can.'

And when she saw the shimmering beauty of the silk, the workmanship, the style, she knew why Claire had taken it home, why those two men were prepared to pay good money for the right to import it directly.

Focus. That was what Guy had said was lacking in the business. And Steven had found it. Too late for him. But not for her.

It was one thing to calmly state that she would go into the bank first thing on Monday morning and demonstrate that she was a responsible adult who was determined to take control of her finances—or lack of them—and her business. And ask for backing to finance her plan.

Quite another to have the bank forestall her with the letter that arrived on Saturday morning, informing her that there were no funds in the account to pay the standing orders, including the one for the rent on the house, and asking her to call in at 10 o'clock on Monday morning to 'discuss' her situation.

She might have wondered if a genuine 'widow' would have been summoned in quite such a peremptory fashion, but, having seen the sum involved, she was too busy wishing that she was alone so that she could have howled with unrestrained fury at yet another blow. Especially when she needed the bank on her side.

Taken by surprise as she'd worked through the post and toyed with some scrambled egg that Connie had forced on her, she'd just had to catch at her breath, bite her lip and be grateful she was sitting down.

'You okay, Fran?'

Maybe she'd caught her breath rather loudly, because Connie stopped emptying the washing machine and turned to look at her. 'Bad news,' she said, without waiting for an answer. 'I make you a nice cup of tea.'

'No. It's fine, really. Nothing,' she said, scooping up the mail and forcing herself to her feet. 'I just need to…'

What?

What could she do?

She found her throat closing with rage, frustration, the need to weep, when she knew she didn't have the time for such luxuries as self-pity. Until today her 'situation', whilst bleak, had not appeared to be so imminently close to disaster. While she couldn't work up much enthusiasm for marketing frogs or lamps she wouldn't give house room, the silk was something else. All night her mind had been running hot with ideas.

She'd been through the recycling box looking

through newspapers—it was too late for magazines—
for the names of the editors of the women's pages.
The ones with the power to put products in front of
millions of eager consumers. Christmas was coming...

She'd still been living in cloud-cuckoo-land, she
realised. Despite the revelations of the past week
she'd been wilfully blind to the size of the disaster
that had overtaken them. It was definitely time to
come down to earth. No matter how hard the landing
might be.

'I'll be upstairs,' she said.

'Okay. It do you good to lie down.'

'No...'

'Toby and I make cakes. We bring you tea when
you wake up.'

'I'll be in the study, Connie,' she said, knowing
that it was useless to argue. Connie was simply trying
to help, but it was going to take a lot more than tea
to fix the mess they were in.

Right now, a miracle would be good, she thought,
gathering up the mail and shutting herself away in the
tiny study.

Then she looked at the glowing silks lying across
the chair. They held out the possibility of a miracle,
but not one that would arrive soon enough to save
her. Save any of them.

'Oh, Steven! Why didn't you bring one of these
home for me? If I'd known...'

But she knew why. Ship the stuff in and ship it out
again before you have to pay for it. That had been
his strategy. It had worked for frogs.

This was different.

But it would have to be her long-term, comeback

strategy. Her future. And Toby's. Right now she needed hard cash, and quickly, or she was going to have to marry Guy to save her family and friends from disaster and what had once been an impossible dream, locked in the deepest recesses of her heart where she never dared go, would become the darkest of nightmares.

Not before she'd examined every other option, she swore. There had to be another way.

She picked up a legal pad, drew a line down the centre, and at the top of one side she wrote 'Assets', and on the other side, 'Liabilities'.

What assets did she have? Her jewellery, mostly. Maybe some of those designer evening gowns could be sold through a dress agency. They had some good pieces of furniture—

Then she realised with another shock that, but for a couple of pieces she'd bought herself, some pictures, she didn't even own that. The house had been furnished when Steven had 'bought' it.

Now all she needed was to find out that the diamonds he'd lavished on her when Toby was born, on their first anniversary in the house, for any excuse, it had seemed, were cubic zirconium and she'd be in the situation Connie had been in before she'd taken her in.

Broke and homeless. Except it wouldn't just be her.

And who would give a damn? Certainly not any of the people they'd socialised with. The women she'd wasted time with at the gym. And when Guy pushed himself into her thoughts, saying, 'I care…', she shoved him right back out again and began on the list of liabilities. It was a relief when the telephone rang, interrupting her.

'Francesca, it's Guy.'

Almost a relief.

For a moment her mouth opened and closed in an attempt to say something. Finally she managed, 'Yes.'

'I'm glad we're both in agreement about that. I wondered if you had any plans for today.'

'I'm sorting out Steven's study,' she said quickly. She needed time, a lot of time, before she could look him in the eye without a blush. 'There's so much to do.'

'Then you won't mind if I take Toby out.'

'Toby?'

Of course, Toby. He wanted to bond with his nephew. Why would he want to take her anywhere? He was going to have to marry...

'To the zoo, or something,' he said.

'The zoo? Oh, *please*!'

'You object? Is that on idealistic grounds? Or are you unhappy with me taking him anywhere? I'd understand, of course. You scarcely know me.'

She knew him. Had known him from the moment she'd set eyes on him. Had been hiding from the fact ever since...

'A fact that doesn't stop you from expecting me to marry you.'

'That's different. Purely business and—'

'And I've done it before. Thanks for reminding me. I hope you'll be easier to divorce.'

There was the slightest pause before he replied. 'Of course. The minute you're back on your feet. It will be a simple matter of annulment for non-consummation.'

Non-consummation.

Well. Great. Why on earth was she hesitating?

'So, what's your objection to the zoo?' he pressed.

'Nothing, I suppose. It's just that it sounds too much like something an every-other-weekend parent would do.' Then, because she'd been abrupt, and because Matty was right, Toby needed a masculine presence in his life, 'You mustn't feel you have to take him out to see him. You're welcome to come here any time.'

'Thank you. I appreciate that, but indulge me for today. I'm new at being an uncle and it was his birthday a few days ago. I understand a treat is mandatory on these occasions. Something involving burgers, ice cream and chocolate?'

'When I mentioned his birthday I didn't mean…'

'I know you didn't. I was well aware of the date. So, is there anything he'd especially like to do?'

'Well, I suppose you could take him on the London Eye. He'd love that.'

'What about you? Would you love it too?' His voice was unexpectedly gentle. 'You could come along and keep an eye on me.'

It was just as well she'd chosen the Eye so she couldn't be tempted to change her mind.

'Wouldn't that rather defeat the object of this male bonding exercise?' Then, as the doorbell chimed, 'Sorry, I've got to go; there's someone at the door. When can we expect you? I don't want to get him over-excited by telling him too soon.'

'I won't be long,' he promised.

She hung up. Sat for a moment, trying to gather herself, then, as the doorbell sounded again Connie shouted, 'You get that please, Fran?'

'No problem.' She leapt to her feet and ran downstairs, flinging back the door.

Guy was leaning against a late model Saab, talking into his cellphone and, as she watched, he put away his wallet, flicked the phone shut and reached into the car to pick up Toby's football. Then he turned and saw her. And, like her, seemed momentarily lost for words.

Then he locked the car and walked up the steps towards her. 'I was beginning to wonder if you'd seen me and made a break for it out the back way,' he said.

'No... It was...'

Toby, hurtling through from the kitchen, rescued her from the necessity of having to say anything. 'Have you come to play f'ball?' he demanded, as she caught him before he could fling himself, covered in cake mixture, into Guy's arms.

'Maybe later,' he replied, crouching down so that he was on Toby's level before handing the ball to him. 'First we're going out to have some fun. If you'd like to?'

'Is Mummy coming, too?'

'Uncle Guy is going to take you on the London Eye, Toby,' Fran said quickly, before Guy could answer him. 'Just the two of you. But not before I've cleaned you up. Come on, upstairs with you.'

'Sure you won't come with us?' Guy said, when she returned with Toby, face shining, hair neatly brushed. 'You look as if you're the one who could do with a break.'

'I may not be wearing black but that doesn't mean I'm ready to—'

'At the very least some fresh air,' he said, cutting off her excuse as if he knew it was just that. An excuse. 'You need to get rid of that sickroom pallor.'

'I can get that sitting peacefully in the garden while you're practising being an uncle. And when you've got the hang of that, take a few years to work on your compliment skills.' Then, quickly, before he was tempted to prove that he could pay a compliment along with the best of them, 'Okay. There are just three rules.' And she went through her 'no' list, ticking them off on her fingers. 'No fizzy drinks. No chocolate. No fries.'

'Are we allowed to laugh?' he asked.

'Okay. Be clever. Give him whatever you want. I just hope you think it's funny when he throws up all over you.'

'No fizzy drinks, no chocolate, no fries. You've got it. Say goodbye to Mummy, Toby,' he said, opening the door.

'Bye, Mummy,' Toby said, looking back suddenly uncertain as Guy lifted him into the back of the car. She wanted to go and snatch him back. Not let him out of her sight.

'Bye, darling,' she said, fixing a reassuring smile to her face. 'I'll see you soon.'

Guy, concentrating on the seatbelt, said, 'Oh, by the way, in case I forget, there'll be a surveyor coming to look at the house some time next week. He'll ring and make an appointment first.'

The blood drained from her face. 'A surveyor?'

He closed the car door, walked around to the driving seat. 'It's nothing to worry about. I took a look at the extension and it seems sound enough, but I'd rather have a structural survey. He'll be able to sort out the planning requirements, too. Among other things.'

'What things?' Fran who, in an effort not to appear

overprotective, had remained at the top of the steps, now wished she'd gone down with them to check the seatbelts, make a nuisance of herself fussing like any decent mother should. 'Why would you care whether the extension is sound or not?' she demanded.

'I care because I've bought the house.'

And with that he got into the car, closed the door and, by the time she'd managed to gain some control over her bottom lip and close her mouth, restart her brain, he was already halfway down the street.

CHAPTER SEVEN

THIS would have been the perfect moment to hail a passing black taxi and say, 'Follow that car!'

Guy couldn't just drop a bombshell like that and then drive away. She wanted an explanation. She wanted to know what the devil he thought he was doing and she wanted to know now!

By some miracle—and she was certainly due one—a cruising taxi appeared just when she needed one and she hailed it. The drama of the moment was somewhat spoiled, however, by the fact that women didn't walk around with wallets in their hip pockets.

Guy's car was long out of sight by the time she'd fetched her bag and she had to content herself with, 'The London Eye, please. As quickly as you can. It's an emergency.'

Even as she said it, she realised how stupid that must sound. What kind of emergency called for a ride on the London Eye? Not that she had any intention of going on it. But the driver—who'd probably heard everything in his time—just said, 'Yes, ma'am', and set off enthusiastically enough in the direction of the huge wheel that carried people high into the sky over the Thames.

Enthusiasm was no match for the slow-moving traffic, however. The meter was moving a lot faster than the taxi and, caught up in a bottleneck at Hyde Park Corner, it occurred to her that she could have got there quicker on the Underground. That she was wasting her time as well as her cash.

Guy and Toby would undoubtedly be five hundred feet above London before she could get there. In fact, the longer she lingered in traffic, the more she was beginning to regret chasing after him. What was she going to do? Berate him in front of the queue for a popular tourist attraction?

And what was she going to say to him anyway? You *can't* buy my house, I won't let you. It wasn't her house and he could do what he damned well pleased. He'd bought an apartment as an investment, why not her house? It had, after all, belonged to his family once, and if he wanted it back it was nothing to do with her.

'This is it, miss,' the driver said.

'What? Oh…' Her desire to reach her destination had waned with every passing click of the taxi meter. She had to go home before she made a complete fool of herself. Think this through calmly…

One look at the fare stopped her from telling the driver to turn around and take her back. In the interests of economy, the return journey would have to be made via public transport and she opened her purse.

'It's okay, I'll get it.'

And this time when she looked up, it wasn't the totally scary 'Eye' looming over her, but Guy, taking charge, paying her fare, opening the door as if he'd been waiting for her. Expecting her. And 'calmly' went right out of the window. Perhaps it was just as well that Toby's, 'Mummy! Uncle Guy said you'd come!' gave her a moment to catch her breath.

'He did?' She looked up. With his back against the

sun, his face was shadowed, unreadable. 'You did?' she demanded.

'It must be difficult letting Toby out of your sight just now. Especially with someone you don't know very well.'

It had been a stupid question, inviting a smug male response, but he was better than that. Kinder, to let her off so lightly. 'I, um, hoped I hadn't let it show.'

'You didn't.'

He just knew?

For a moment she felt warmed by his understanding. Then reality caught up with her. 'Are you telling me that what you said about the house was just a ruse to get me to follow you?'

She couldn't decide whether to be relieved or infuriated by that but before she could make up her mind he said, 'So what took you so long? Come on, we're ready to go.'

She glanced up at the wheel. 'Already? I thought you'd have to queue.'

'I phoned ahead and booked while you were taking your time about answering the front door.'

Toby caught at her hand and began dragging her towards the boarding area. 'Come *on*, Mummy!'

'Oh, but I don't have a ticket,' she protested, digging in her heels.

'I booked three.' *Oh, right. Now he was a smug male…* 'It'll do you good,' he assured her in the most maddening way. 'In fact, I believe you've already got a little more colour in your cheeks.'

She didn't doubt it. But it had nothing to do with fresh air.

Restrained by her son's presence, she couldn't say

the word she was thinking, but she gave Guy a look that would have left him in no doubt. He just grinned.

And took her breath away.

He'd smiled at her before. Once, twice, maybe, when Steven had introduced her. Restrained things that hadn't reached his eyes. As if from the beginning he'd disapproved.

This was something else.

'Come on,' he said impatiently, as she remained glued to the spot. 'You know you want to ask me about the house. Once we're aboard you'll have me at your mercy.'

'Ple-e-e-ease, Mummy!'

The combination was lethal. How could she possibly say no?

It would be okay if she didn't look down, she told herself, as she allowed herself to be ushered into the capsule along with the rest of the group. So long as she didn't stand up, kept her eyes on the distant horizon, she'd be fine. The trick was not to look down. Not even to *think* about looking down...

Toby ran straight to the far end of the bubble so that he could see everything. 'Oh, wow!' he said. Then, 'Look, Uncle Guy! Look, Mummy!'

So much for sitting on the bench in the middle, as far away from the 'view' as possible. At least she didn't have to speak. Guy pointed out the sights as, slowly, they began to rise, allowing her to turn her back on it as if she was more interested in something far in the distance on the opposite side.

Realising that Toby didn't want facts, that all he wanted to do was look, Guy turned to her. Perhaps it was her white face, her even whiter knuckles, that gave him the clue that she wasn't entirely comfortable. Or maybe he just wanted to give her the chance to talk.

Whatever the reason, he took her arm and said, 'Let's go and sit down.'

'But Toby…'

'He's fine.'

Intellectually she knew that. But intellect had nothing to do with a fear of heights.

'Ask me about the house,' Guy said, as he eased out her clenched fingers and led her across to the bench, keeping her hand between his as he sat beside her. 'It's why you came.'

'Is it? I thought it was because I was a fretful mother.' He didn't reply. Fair enough. They both knew it was a delaying tactic. A putting-it-off moment because she didn't want to know what he'd done. Whatever it was would be wrong. 'Well, have you?' she asked irritably. 'Bought it?'

'It's your home. Now it's safe.'

Oh, good grief, he had!

'And, I promise you, you'll hardly know I'm there.'

'There?' She caught a glimpse of the Thames dropping away from them, felt a familiar sickening lurch in her stomach. This was more important. 'What do you mean, *there*?'

'That's the "among other things" I mentioned. I'm going to convert the attic into a small self-contained apartment to use when I'm in London.'

About to demand to know what gave him the right to think he could do any such thing, she checked herself. He'd bought the house. He had every right. Since her mouth was open and she had to say something, she said, 'Won't it be a bit of a squeeze after the Thames-side loft conversion with every luxury?'

'I won't miss it,' he assured her.

'Miss it?' *Miss it?* 'Are you telling me that you've sold it?' she demanded. She'd assumed he was simply increasing his property portfolio. Using the opportunity to let the loft conversion at some fabulous rent. And the sinking sensation in her stomach had nothing to do with her fear of heights. 'Please don't tell me you've had to sell it to buy the house?'

'I wish I didn't have to force myself on you in this way.' He didn't look exactly distraught, but then he'd as good as admitted he hated the place. Even so… 'Fortunately, I'm not around that much.'

'Wouldn't it just be cheaper to pay the rent until I get myself sorted out? If you're that worried about Toby being homeless?'

'It isn't just Toby, though. Is it?'

'Steven wouldn't expect you to take care of Matty and Connie.'

'He asked me to take care of you and Toby. It seems to me you're all a package and it really is easier to do it this way.'

It certainly would be no simple matter rehousing Matty…

'But you could have just renewed the lease.' She didn't want him to have bought the house, she discovered. That was too…personal.

'That was my first thought,' he said. 'There's no easy way to tell you this, Francesca, but your landlord gave Steve six months notice to quit four months ago. You only had a couple of months before you'd have had to move out.'

Surprisingly, she didn't feel any huge sense of shock. The revelations of the last week had taken her beyond any place where she could feel shocked.

Steven had known he was on borrowed time, that there was nothing he could do to put things right. Her only regret was that she hadn't overridden his insistence that she shouldn't send for Guy sooner. In time.

She couldn't find it in her heart to blame him for lying to her, even when he had been dying. Keeping up the pretence. There was no point. He was gone and all she could think about was the stress he must have been under. Keeping up the front of a successful businessman. The doting husband and father. The lavish gifts. Never letting it show. For months…years…

No wonder he'd been so adamant that she need never get involved with finances. It was the last thing he had wanted.

'Poor Steven,' she said at last. 'How he must have suffered. No wonder he asked you to marry me. He obviously couldn't think of anything else to do.'

Guy blenched. The compassion in her voice sliced deep into the hope buried so deep within him that he had dared not acknowledge it.

Despite everything, she couldn't bring herself to blame his brother for the magnitude of the disaster he'd brought on her. She should be railing against what he'd done to her. Instead she felt empathy.

Any hope that one day she might recover from her loss sufficiently to see him as anything other than Steve's disapproving brother was dealt a mortal blow.

'Do you think that the stress might have been a factor in his death?' she asked. 'He went down so fast. I did ask him if I should get in touch with you, but we all thought he'd have more time. At the time I was just grateful he didn't linger, suffer more, but—'

'Francesca,' he said, desperate to stop her blaming

herself. 'There was nothing you could have done. His charm, his persuasiveness, were his greatest gifts. He fooled me more times than I can remember.' Had fooled him into parting with a 'deposit' for the house. 'Believe me, he was irresistible and he knew it.'

She almost smiled. 'There's no need to be kind.'

'Not kind. Realistic. You've nothing to blame yourself for.'

She looked at him for a moment. Then nodded. 'Thank you.' Then, 'I'm sorry you've been dragged into this mess. You really don't have to buy the house. We'll manage somehow.'

'It's—'

'And don't tell me you've bought it already. It takes weeks, months to buy and sell property.'

'Most of it spent with the papers sitting in some lawyer's pending tray. Tom Palmer has a century of papers on that house. Nothing has changed in the last ten years—'

'Except the extension.'

'Except the extension,' he agreed. 'Fortunately, the owner didn't know about that, or it might have caused you some problems. As it is I'll have to sort it out with the planning people.'

'No. It didn't need planning permission. Steven said…' She stopped. 'Oh, great.'

He reached out, lightly touched her hand. Immediately withdrew it when she jumped as if scalded. 'Forget it,' he said abruptly. The only way this would work was if she thought him completely oblivious. Just doing his duty… 'It's done. Your home is safe and you can stop worrying about what's going to happen to Matty and Connie and the stray cat. You've been through enough.'

'How did you know about the stray cat?'

'Give me some credit for imagination. You've got everything else. And, since you were denied the rescue dog, there had to be a stray cat.'

Guy didn't sound particularly impressed and she didn't blame him. Was that the way it had always been? Steven messing up. Guy bailing him out.

'You can't do this, Guy,' she said. And she wasn't just talking about the house. 'I won't let you.'

'It isn't in your power to stop me, Francesca. Besides, as I said, it's already done.'

'You can't have exchanged contracts.'

'I can and I have. All that was required was the finance and the will.'

She knew she should be grateful, but she wasn't. She was just angry. 'This is stupid. We are not your responsibility.' She looked up at him, trying to read his face. Nothing. He seemed to be able to lock down his emotions. Keep them hidden. 'What did Steven say in that letter he left you?' A lot more than was in the not-really-a-codicil to his will she was certain.

'He was concerned about Toby. That's all.'

It came out so easily that she had the feeling that, anticipating the question, he'd rehearsed his answer.

It wasn't all. She could see from his eyes that it was far from all. And from the set of his jaw that he wasn't going to tell her any more.

'You must see that it's the sensible solution for everyone,' he continued. 'I don't need a vast apartment sitting empty half the time. You need a home for Toby and everyone. And you needn't worry about the future, either. With Steve dead I had to make a new will. I've left everything to you.'

'Guy…' Her voice caught in her throat.

'I find it's the things you don't allow for that catch you out.'

Every time, she thought.

She thought she'd met Prince Charming, was having his baby, had thought that life was going to be happy ever after.

Then she'd walked through the door of a restaurant and discovered that life wasn't that simple.

It had been an illusion, of course. That moment when she'd looked at Guy Dymoke and had a momentary vision of what 'happy ever after' really meant. It had been over so quickly that she had managed to fool herself into believing that she'd imagined it. It hadn't been difficult. Seconds later she couldn't believe he was the same man. He'd been so distant, cold, living up to Steven's description so completely that she'd managed to put the moment behind her. Which was just as well. She was already on a path from which there was no turning back.

Except that Steven had lied. Lied about himself. Lied about his brother. And she had lied, too. The only part of their relationship that wasn't a lie, it seemed, was Toby. She looked at the sturdy little boy standing a few feet away from her, completely absorbed by something below them.

'Don't leave your estate to me. Leave it to Toby,' she said, when she'd recovered sufficiently to speak. 'He's your heir. At least for now.'

'You are his mother. You will take care of him. And as my wife you can inherit everything without the Chancellor taking his cut.'

'Oh, please! You're not seriously going to marry me as a tax avoidance measure?'

'If I fell under Matty's metaphorical bus, you'd

have to sell the house to pay inheritance tax. This way makes more sense.'

'It makes sense if you haven't got a heart, but since we're talking about the unexpected, let's really go for it.' She looked at him, demanding a response.

'What's on your mind?'

'This. We get married. You live upstairs in your little apartment. Me and Lame Ducks Incorporated are spread out all over the rest of your house. That's what you have in mind, right?'

'Right.'

'Okay. Now tell me this. What happens when you meet the girl of your dreams and fall in love?'

Fran had to ask the question, even though the very idea of him falling in love drove daggers through her.

'That's the one thing that isn't going to happen, Francesca.'

His conviction shook her momentarily, but she pressed on. 'Guy, I know you spend most of your life in the wilderness, chipping lumps off rock looking for oil and minerals—'

'Really it's a bit more technical than that,' he objected.

'—but you do return to civilisation occasionally. And please don't try to kid me that you're gay. That wasn't a submarine I saw in the bath…'

Oh, sugar! Blushing furiously, she found herself trying to shovel the words back in with her tongue, covering her hot face with her hands.

He didn't say a word. He didn't even make some snippy comment about getting some 'colour in her cheeks'. He said, 'It isn't going to happen, Francesca.' She frowned, forgetting her embarrassment. 'I've already met the only woman I ever wanted to marry. She was in love with someone else.'

She knew without question that he wasn't trying to make it easy for her. He was telling her the plain, unvarnished truth. And because she knew instinctively that, for him, love once given would be given for ever, she felt something, some small spark of hope, die inside her.

And all she could say was, 'I'm so sorry. I had no idea.'

'I've learned to live with it and Steve knew. That's why he asked me to marry you. It's no big deal, and this way if I do fall off a mountain or get eaten by a crocodile, you're taken care of. I can go away without having to worry about you or Toby.'

How ironic. How perfect. They were both in love with someone who could never return their love. They were the ideal couple.

'So? Can I go ahead and confirm the arrangements?'

'What?' Then, 'Oh, yes. I suppose so,' she said, finally surrendering to the inevitable. 'When did you have in mind?'

'As soon as possible.'

She took in a deep breath.

'There's no point in waiting. It's purely a business arrangement. I promise you won't find me in your bath—with or without submarine—on a regular basis.'

That's what was so terrible. If it had been unbridled passion there would be some excuse...

'Steven is scarcely cold in his grave,' she protested.

'It was his idea,' he reminded her.

'He was dying. Desperate.'

Whoever he was in love with was wise to steer well clear, she thought. This man could break your heart without even trying. To know that he loved someone else was difficult enough…

'This is madness,' she said. 'Impossible.'

'You said that about buying the house. Actually marriage is a lot easier. Nowhere near so much paperwork. Just ten minutes of your time and a couple of witnesses. But why am I telling you? You've married for convenience before and, unlike your last husband, I'm not going to disappear and cause you endless problems.'

'No, you're going to stick around and cause them.'

'Not even that.' Before she could say the words exploding on her tongue he went on, 'The registrar is free the Thursday after next. Eleven-fifteen. There's no need to dress up for the occasion.'

He had never doubted that she would say yes.

'I realise it's very short notice, but I don't have much time. I'm flying back the same evening.'

'Back?'

'I still have a job to do.'

'I understand why you're going. I was just hoping for rather more detail. As your wife I think I'm entitled to at least be given a little more information than which side of some distant continent you'll be living in, don't you?'

He told her exactly where he was going.

'But…isn't there a civil war going on there?'

'You read the newspapers. Good, I don't have to explain the risks, why I need to tie up the loose ends before I go, why I have to go myself.'

'Because everyone else has a family? What are we?' He didn't have to answer. A nuisance. An inconvenience. A burden. 'Please, Guy. Leave it. No one should be going into that situation.'

'You'd be a wealthy widow.'

'Is that what you think I want?' She stood up, quite suddenly unable to bear being so close to him. Unable to bear the way he could make a gesture that was fine and noble sound cheap. 'Go to hell, Guy!'

Unable to even look at him, she turned away, at which point she realised that only the children were watching the view. The rest of the passengers were too busy earwigging their conversation to bother about the panorama of London, the surrounding counties laid out beneath them.

Fortunately Toby, who'd been staring, silent and rapt, at the view as they'd risen slowly up into the sky suddenly shouted, 'Look, Mummy! There's a ship!'

And, desperate for any distraction, she looked.

For a moment she only saw the river curving away towards Tower Bridge and the grey bulk of *HMS Belfast* looking like a toy battleship. Then reality kicked in.

She was standing in mid-air with nothing to hold on to, and marriage, convenient or otherwise, was the last thing on her mind.

'Oh, no…' She clawed at the air, in desperation for a handhold. 'Oh, please…'

Guy was at her side in an instant, blocking out the terror with the solidity of his chest, holding her anchored safely in his arms until the panic subsided. Only then did he ease back, help her to the seat in the centre of the bubble. But he still didn't let go, holding her against his shoulder, blocking out the sickening emptiness.

'I'm sorry,' he murmured into her hair, so close that it felt like a kiss. 'I'm so sorry. Why didn't you say? Idiot…'

She didn't say anything, just stayed there, tucked up safely against Guy's chest, while her pulse gradually slowed to match the slow, steady thud of his heart.

Then Toby came and wriggled up beside them and Guy put out an arm to scoop him up close.

Holding them all safe.

'Do you have the rings?'

Rings! She hadn't thought…

But of course Guy had. He produced a pair of simple, classic matching wedding rings from his pocket and placed them on the velvet cushion in front of them. Then he picked up the smaller of the pair, took her hand and, placing it on her finger, said 'I call upon these persons here present to witness that I, Guy Edward Dymoke, take Francesca Elizabeth Lang as my lawful wedded wife…'

As she listened to Guy's low, firm voice clearly affirm his vow, Fran couldn't believe she was doing this. It had taken her five years to extricate herself from her first 'marriage of convenience'. An annoyingly inconvenient marriage, as it had turned out, but at least she'd been able to tell herself that her motives had been good.

She'd almost managed to convince herself this time, too. She wasn't marrying for her own benefit, but to protect Toby, Matty, Connie. But definitely not the stray cat. Even she wasn't that much of a fool.

Except that now, standing beside him, her hand clasped firmly in his, she knew that she was every inch a fool. She wasn't just doing this to keep a roof over her family's head, but for herself. Hoping against hope that her marriage to Guy would somehow evolve from an upmarket house share, a fiscal convenience, into something much more. Something real and true.

She realised the registrar was looking at her expectantly. 'I call upon these persons here present,' he prompted, as if he'd said it before.

Fran opened her mouth, but she couldn't speak. Couldn't go through with it. It was a lie. False. She couldn't do it again. Must not do it.

She began to breathe much too fast as panic swept over her, certain that at any minute someone would burst into the room and expose her, expose them both as frauds.

'Francesca?' Guy's face was grave, his eyes steady as a rock. And then, as if he could read her mind, he gently squeezed her hand as if saying, *It's okay. I understand. You're not doing this for yourself...*

And finally she picked up the larger ring, her heart hammering hot and fast in her chest. She felt dizzy, light-headed, her voice seeming to come from a long way off as she placed it on his finger and slowly repeated the words. Carefully weighing each one, she began, 'I call upon these persons here present...to witness that I, Francesca Elizabeth Lang...take Guy Edward Dymoke to be my lawful wedded husband...'

She'd done this before, but on that occasion only her head had been engaged. This time it was important. This time she meant it and maybe that did make it all right.

Because, even if he never knew it, she was making a true vow with her whole heart.

Then it was done and she was looking up at Guy,

forcing herself to look as if this was just another meaningless ten-minute wedding, her expression saying nothing more than, *Okay, what next?*

It was the registrar who answered her unspoken question as he smiled and said, 'You may kiss the bride.'

No... Yes... There was an agonising pause that seemed to go on for ever before Guy bent, touched his lips to hers.

They clung momentarily to hers, scorching not just her body but her soul until she thought she would faint—but whether from joy or from despair she could not have said as, with a little gasp, she drew back before she betrayed herself.

The kiss was for the registrar, to add the mask of reality to the pretence, nothing more. As Guy had so regularly reminded her, she'd done this before. A kiss was no big deal. And then, nineteen years old and with ideals rather than love burning in her heart, it hadn't been.

This time they felt like the most solemn, the most important words she had ever uttered.

Unable to look at him, deal with the absence of any emotional response, she left him to sign the register, turning instead to the two women who'd abandoned their computer terminals for ten minutes to act as witnesses, to thank them. Blushing like any ordinary bride as she accepted their congratulations.

'Francesca?' Guy handed her the pen and she added her own shaky signature to the book as he took the certificate that made her, officially, Mrs Guy Dymoke, tucked it away in his inside jacket pocket and thanked the registrar as he added his good wishes for their future happiness. Then Guy took her arm and led her, almost fainting, outside to the steps of the Town Hall.

CHAPTER EIGHT

'FRANCESCA? Are you all right?'

She shook her head, unable to answer, as she took in huge gasps of air.

'Take your time.'

'I'm sorry. That was...' She didn't even attempt to finish the sentence. There wasn't a word to express the way she was feeling. To have the one thing you most wanted in the world. Yet not have it. To know that you could never have it.

'I know,' he said.

'No, Guy,' she said. 'I promise you, you don't.'

His gaze met hers and for one brief, shocking moment she saw his pain. Remembered the woman he loved but could never have because she loved someone else. And she laid her hand on his arm.

'I'm so sorry. You deserve better from me than that.'

He looked down at her hand, pale against his sleeve, and the bright new gold of the wedding ring gleamed as it caught the sun.

'I do understand how hard it must have been for you. I wish there had been more time.'

'It wouldn't have made any difference.'

'No. I suppose not,' he said, apparently missing her allusion to his own unattainable love. Then, 'I'm surprised you didn't bring Matty and Connie with you. As witnesses.'

She let it go, allowed him to take her hand, walk

her to his car, open the door for her, ease her into the passenger seat.

'I didn't tell them,' she said, as he slid behind the wheel. She was already missing his hand in hers. The warmth of it. The strength of it. 'About this. I don't want them to feel...' She stopped, unable to say the word. But he had no problems filling the void.

'Guilty?' He started the car, pulled out into the traffic.

'Responsible. All I've told them is that you've bought the house and will be moving into the top floor flat when it's been converted.'

'And they've accepted that?'

Fran recalled the look of relief on her cousin's face. Uncharacteristically, she hadn't asked what was going on. Grateful that she'd avoided a difficult interrogation, she hadn't elaborated. Matty, she realised belatedly, hadn't asked because she hadn't wanted to be told anything she didn't want to hear.

'You only went through with this for them, didn't you?' he said. 'Nothing else would have persuaded you.'

She glanced across at him. He was concentrating on the traffic and all she had was his hard, unyielding profile. She wondered what he'd do if she told him the truth. Recoil in horror, in all probability... 'What would you have done if I'd said no?'

'It was Steve's dying request. I don't think you'd have denied him anything, let alone that.' For a moment he met her gaze head-on. Then, as the traffic moved, 'And, even if you were inclined to, I wasn't about to let it happen.'

'No?' she challenged him. 'No, of course you weren't. Steven told me that you'd only backed down once before in your entire life. What was it, Guy? A charging rhino?'

'Something equally obdurate,' he assured her. 'The human heart.' She stared at him. The woman he'd loved? He'd walked away? Let her go without a fight? 'Something that isn't involved on this occasion,' he said so coldly that she shivered. Then, as they were temporarily halted at the lights, he turned to look at her. 'Which is why I wasn't prepared to take no for an answer, Mrs Dymoke.'

And she knew he'd added the 'Mrs Dymoke' just to demonstrate how obdurate he could be.

'It's Miss Lang,' she snapped back at him. 'It will always be Miss Lang...'

She looked down at the circle of polished gold around her finger. It was bright and pure, a burning a brand on her finger, and she tugged at it, desperate to be rid of it. Wrenching at it when it refused to slide over her knuckle.

After a moment he pulled up and closed his hand over hers, stopping her. 'Leave it, Francesca.' And for a moment something in his voice made her look up, made her hope... 'You'll hurt yourself,' he said, removing his hand as if stung.

And realising that she was just fooling herself, she gave the ring another tug, just to show him that she didn't care how much it hurt, she just wanted to be free of it. 'It's too damned tight,' she declared, ignoring the fact that it had slipped on as if made for her.

'It'll come off easily enough with some soap when you get home.'

'There is no way I'm going home wearing this!' His head went back, as if she'd punched him on the jaw. 'I don't want Matty or Connie to know,' she said, pleading with him to see. Wishing she hadn't said it. He was only doing what he thought was right. For the best. He had no way of knowing... 'It's so soon...after Steven. They wouldn't understand.'

'No? I believe they would. I think they have more faith in you than you have in yourself.' And for a moment it was there again. An unexpected gentleness... 'But it's your business, not mine. And, speaking of business...' He leaned across her, opened the glove box and took out a large envelope. 'These are your new credit cards. Everything you'll need.'

'But...'

'Why don't you indulge yourself in a little retail therapy? Treat yourself to lunch in Harvey Nicks or Claibournes? I'm sure their powder room will supply all the soap you need to wash away the last hour,' he said.

'Don't! Please! I can't bear it.'

When she didn't take the envelope, he said, 'You're my wife. Whatever I have is yours,' he said, brushing away a tear that had spilled on to her cheek. 'Take it.'

For a moment they seemed so close. She felt as if all she had to do was reach out to bridge the chasm, go into his arms.

'I really do have to go,' he said, dropping the envelope into her lap. And the gulf was wider than ever.

'Go?' Fran forgot all about her desperation to remove his ring, her hurt at his suggestion that she might even consider doing anything as mindless as shopping. 'Go where?' she asked. Then, realising that he meant *go*, get on a plane, fly away to the other side of the world, 'So soon? Without saying goodbye to Toby or Matty?'

'I said my goodbyes yesterday. While you were at the office.'

'They didn't tell me.' It was as well that her eyes were already full of tears. 'Toby was very quiet last night. I should have known something had upset him.'

'I promised him that I'd come back as soon as I could.'

'You'd damn well better—' She fought back the sob in her voice. There was no reason in the world for her to cry. This was a marriage of convenience. No heart involved. He'd said so. 'Small boys don't understand when people go away and don't come back,' she said. 'I've told him his Daddy is with Jesus, but I'm afraid he thinks it's just like one of his business trips. That he'll be back after a week or two.'

Guy was dying inside. He felt torn in half. In one moment he'd gained the one thing he had wanted most in the world. And lost it. He'd actually planned to take her to lunch, spin out for as long as possible the moment when she wore his ring, when he could make believe that she was his. But he couldn't do it. Not after the kiss he should have resisted had burned itself into his brain so that he could think of nothing else. He could only pray that it would replace the dream that had haunted him for so long, because it was all he'd have of her.

She'd loved Steve. Stayed with him. Had been prepared to commit herself to him for life. Even now she didn't blame him for what he'd done to her. Only pitied him, blamed herself.

His plane didn't leave until early evening, but the

sooner he put himself safely on the far side of the check-in barrier the better.

'I won't let Toby down,' he said. 'You have my word.'

She blinked, looked away, out of the window and up at the apartment block, then out across the Thames.

'Is this where you live?' she asked.

'Lived. Someone will pick up the few things I'm sending over to Elton Street. If you'll store them until the conversion is done?'

'Oh, yes, of course.'

'I just have to pick up my bags, then drop the keys in at the office. You can take the car, keep it,' he said, handing her the keys. 'It's insured for you to drive.'

'But how are you getting to the airport?' she asked. Then, not waiting for him to tell her, she opened the door and got out. 'What am I saying? I'll take you.' She forced a smile. 'That's what wives do, isn't it?'

Guy, quite unable to help himself, looked at her across the roof of the car and said, 'You might not want to go into what wives do, Francesca.' Then, taking pity on her as she blushed, he said, 'It's okay. I really don't expect you to morph into the perfect wife. There is, after all, no one either of us has to convince and I really can't see you as the kind of woman who'd get up at the crack of dawn every morning to run her man to the station every morning with her coat over her pyjamas.'

'Don't you?'

She was wearing a pale grey designer suit, sexy high-heeled shoes and her pale hair swept up in the height of sophistication. Steve had turned her into his ideal. The kind of woman who never had to wash a dish or iron his shirt. Just look good and display his success to the world. But her eyes told a different story and oh, dear God, yes he could see her all too clearly, hair mussed, no make-up, soft, warm and with the imprint of his body still on hers…

He was nearing the end of his tether.

He'd been through an emotional bombardment. Swearing death-us-do-part commitment to the woman he loved, while having to convince her that it meant nothing more to him than honouring a debt to his dead brother, had taken a painful toll because, unlike Francesca, he'd meant it. Every word. She couldn't wait to see the back of him, while he was wrecked at the thought of leaving them, leaving her, and he knew, just knew, that Steve was looking on somewhere, watching, laughing, saying 'Got you!' as he taunted him with what he most desired, all the while knowing that it was impossible for him to take it.

He'd only fully understood how difficult it would be since that moment on the 'Eye' when she'd surrendered briefly, let him hold her safe and, in the most bittersweet of moments, he'd realised that he'd both won and lost.

That she would marry him for the sake of her family, no other reason. That any chance of allowing her time to grieve, to come to see him as someone special, someone she might in time grow to love, was lost to him.

The minute money had become the prime force of their relationship, any hope of emotional commitment had to be put on hold. How could he reveal his feelings now because she wouldn't know for certain that he was being sincere. That he wasn't simply making the best of a bad job and expecting more than a paper marriage for his money?

And it worked two ways. If she surrendered, he'd never be sure if it was because she felt she had no choice.

He was going to have to sit it out. Wait. Prove himself over however long it took and maybe one day she would trust him enough. Feel enough. He could do it. He'd lived three years without hope. Now he had the faint glimmer of a possibility of a future, he was prepared to wait a lifetime...

So, instead of foisting himself upon her, he'd spent time with Toby, visited Matty, eaten the food that Connie had insisted on cooking for him—whether he had wanted it or not. Made friends, allies, of all of them. But he'd given Francesca all the room she had clearly needed. Even the most thick-skinned of men couldn't have failed to get the message that, having agreed to marry him, she was doing everything she could to avoid him.

Why else would she spend all her time in an office that wasn't doing any business? How much clearing up could there be?

But right now all this careful reasoning meant nothing. He wanted to kick something, take out his rage on some inanimate object, howl like a wounded animal. He was having to wear a civilised front, behave like a man unmoved by anything or anyone when he'd never felt so close to exploding.

The truth was that he couldn't bear another minute of her sitting beside him, her scent seeping into his skin, her hair, sleek and smooth, a blatant invitation to a man to pull at the pins, let it loose.

She did something to him that no other woman had ever managed. Robbed him of reason.

He'd believed he could do this, but he'd been right to stay away all these years. He should never have come back.

Not that he imagined it had been easy for Francesca, either. She'd just lost the man she loved— a man she'd forgiven every kind of betrayal—and he'd sensed her struggle, felt her hand trembling in his as she'd nearly failed at the last minute, barely able to get out the words. Seen her distress as, outraged at his apparent carelessness, she'd tried to tear off the ring he'd put on her finger and throw it back at him. And his heart broke for her. Broke all over again for himself.

'It really isn't necessary to take me to the airport,' he said abruptly, wishing he'd handled this differently. It had seemed so simple. Drive to the apartment, hand over the car keys, say goodbye. No emotion. No fuss. But nothing in this situation was simple, and there were no self-help guides on how to avoid the pitfalls. He was on his own and it was a steep learning curve. 'I'll take a cab to the office and someone will run me in from there.'

'Your secretary?'

'She's rather more than that,' he said. And, picking up an edge to her voice, 'Does it matter?'

'Is she pretty?'

'Catherine?' He looked at her more closely. A definite edge. She was jealous? Why? And, because he was human, he said, 'She's tall, blond and sensational.' Which was the truth. She was tall and blond— although he imagined that mainly due to the intervention of science—and she was a sensational administrator. 'You know, you're beginning to sound like a jealous wife,' he said. And, since he felt much too good about that, he punctured his own ego with, 'Were you like this with Steve?'

She looked at the ring he'd placed on her finger, then raised those sinfully long lashes and said, 'I wasn't married to him, Guy. Maybe I'd better get this off before I completely lose the plot.' And, when he didn't leap to agree, 'I imagine you do have some soap in your apartment? Or is everything packed?'

Left with little choice but to run the swipe card through the lock on the entrance, he held the door for her and summoned the lift. The doors slid open immediately and they were whisked, in silence, to the top floor.

And then, as she stood in the entrance to the vast living room, it seemed that she was the one lost for words.

Fran had never doubted that Guy was wealthy. Steven had told her often enough that he was and the fact that he could raise the finance to buy her house at a day's notice proved it beyond all doubt. But the apartment, expensively understated, elegant, beautiful beyond anything she could have imagined, rammed the point home. This wasn't the home of a man who was just wealthy. This was the home of a man who was seriously rich.

The softest leather furniture invited the weary to relax and be cosseted. Richly coloured oriental rugs were laid on pale, polished floors. Books and fine paintings adorned the walls.

Guy had told her that this was just a convenient place for him to stay during his brief visits to London. An investment. Maybe that was what it had become,

but that wasn't how it had been originally perceived.
This was the home of a man who'd put thought and
care into it. It was a place to share with someone.
And she knew, instinctively, that this had been furnished with the woman he loved in mind.

No wonder he'd been so reluctant to let her see it.
If she'd known he had to surrender this to pay
Steven's debts, buy the house—and he must have
done or why else would he be converting her attic
into a tiny little self-contained flat for himself?—she
would have... What? Refused to allow it? He'd said,
just minutes ago, that he wasn't going to take no for
an answer.

Guy didn't join her, but remained on the far side
of the wide double doors as she toured the room,
touching the spine of a leather-bound book, gazing at
a painting, not quite able to come to terms with the
fact that he had something of such value simply hanging on his wall. Trying to get inside his head. Trying
to imagine the woman who had inspired such adora-
tion. Trying to make it all add up.

'I'll get my bags,' he said.

'No!' She turned to face him. 'What have you
done, Guy?' He didn't answer. 'This is a world away
from the way you described it to me. It's a home. Full
of beautiful things.'

'I didn't say it was ugly. Just not what I need any
more.'

'And you've sold it? Just like that? To buy my
house?'

'Francesca—'

He was going to lie to her. He wasn't as good at
it as Steven. One minute he was looking straight at

her, the next he was more interested in one of the paintings...

'Please give me credit for some sense, Guy,' she said, before he could. Then, with a gesture at the single box, the small trunk, all he was taking with him, she said, 'The pictures are worth a fortune. That one alone would have done it.'

And she waited.

Finally he said, 'Yes, it probably would. You're right, of course. I haven't sold the flat. I've let as it stands to an American bank for one of their senior vice-presidents.'

'Let it?' she repeated. 'Let it?' She looked around. 'With all this priceless...stuff?'

'Believe me, the rental reflects the value of contents as well as the accommodation.'

'But...why?'

'I told you. I bought this as an investment and it's done well. I've tripled my capital outlay. Something that Steve could have done if he'd used the money I gave him wisely. I should have let it before, of course. It's a terrible waste of resources leaving it empty and it put the insurance premiums through the roof. The apartment in Elton Street will be much more cost effective.'

Money? Was that all this meant to him? She didn't believe it for a minute.

'I meant why did you lie to me?'

'I didn't. You assumed I had to sell and I didn't deny it.'

'Why?' she persisted.

Because he was a fool, Guy told himself. Because he wanted to be able to help her in every way, put all of his resources at her command, give her not just a home, but everything she'd ever need. Because he loved her.

None of them were reasons he could offer for what must now seem completely irrational behaviour. Whatever he said was going to make a bad situation worse, but he wasn't going to add his unwanted passion to her burden. It was too soon after Steve's death. Even if, by some miracle, she returned his feelings, she would deny it. She could do nothing else.

'Guilt is the best arm-twister I know,' he said, distancing himself from his voice, his actions. Her confused expression as she silently mouthed the word back at him.

'Guilt?'

'Steve taught me that. You're right, of course. I could easily have bought the house, given it to you, but I needed you to marry me.'

'Needed?'

'Yes,' he said, knowing that he was breaking every tiny link he'd forged with her in the last few days. Destroying her memories of those moments when they'd been close. Smashing every one of his dreams beyond any hope of repair with each word he uttered. He'd tied her to him out of his own longings, hoped that he could one day win her affection, her trust, her love. Now he was giving her the freedom to hate him for it. Releasing her from any need for gratitude.

'This might be a good moment to tell you that Tom Palmer is sorting out adoption papers for Toby. It's just a formality. I simply want to be sure that when you move on, find someone new, I'll have some family rights. That he won't just disappear from my life. Fortunately he won't have to change his name.'

'Find someone new? Are you mad? Steven has

been dead less than a month!' Then, frowning, 'Is that what was in Steven's letter?'

How easy it would be to lie. Blame Steve. 'No, he didn't think of it. But then I always did have a better grasp of reality than my brother and Toby is all the family I've got.' All the family he was ever likely to have. 'Don't even think of trying to fight me on it, Francesca. And if you do think about it remember your responsibilities and leave well alone.'

'You bastard!'

'Yes, well, Steve did tell you. You should have listened to him.'

'You can't do this,' she said, floundering in a mixture of outrage and helplessness. Every atom of his being reached out to her, yearned to reassure her, but he held his ground. 'I'll...I'll have the marriage annulled,' she declared.

'On what grounds? You're going to find it rather difficult to prove it wasn't consummated unless I cooperate. And I will, but only when I have what I want.'

'You think I'm prepared to wait? I'm going straight back to the registrar. Tell him the truth...' And she headed for the door.

All Guy wanted was to stop her looking at the pictures he'd bought because he'd known, instinctively, that she would love them as he did. Touching the books he wanted to share with her. Running her hand along the back of the huge sofa that was big enough for two people to lie in each other's arms as they watched the setting sun suffuse the sky with soft pinks and mauves.

He wanted to stop her asking questions that he couldn't answer without betraying himself.

Wanted to make her angry enough to walk out, leave him, so that he could gather himself, restore the outward calm. But not like this. He couldn't let her leave like this.'

'Francesca, wait—'

She pushed past him, refusing to stop, refusing to listen and, in desperation, he caught at her sleeve.

She was moving faster than he'd realised and, as he grabbed her, she spun around, almost losing her balance on her high heels. Would have done if he hadn't caught her, held her.

'Don't…'

She was breathing heavily, flushed, and her hair had broken free of the restraining pins. She looked distraught, as if she was hurting so deeply that noth-ing could make it better, and tears filled her eyes as she stood there, powerless, his unwilling captive bride. But she wasn't surrendering. She lifted her chin, lifted her hands to capture the loose strands that curled about her face, as if somehow she could restore her dignity by anchoring her hair smoothly back in place.

But as she raised her lashes to stare him down, met his gaze head on, it was as if time had slipped side-ways to another place. And her eyes, which a second earlier had been as cold as steel, melted, darkened…

Neither of them spoke. She just let her hair fall and it tumbled loose about her face, her shoulders, gold in the autumn sunlight slanting in from the skylight above them. He might have been dreaming, except that when he reached up to cradle her cheek he could feel the warmth of her skin against his palm, his fin-gers. When he tightened his hold on her waist, her body moulded into his as if they had been made to fit. And when he lowered his mouth to hers, her lips parted, hot, honey-sweet, everything he'd ever dreamed of.

He'd lived this moment over and over in his imagination. Knew exactly how it would be. The way he'd pick her up and carry her to his bed, undress her slowly, taking his time as he explored every part of her with his hands, his mouth, his tongue, until she was crying out for him. Until he could wait no longer to claim her. In his head, his heart, he knew it would be precious and beautiful and something neither of them would ever forget, no matter what happened afterwards.

The reality was the swift, explosive and purely physical coupling of two people in desperate need. No sweet words, no forever promises, nothing gentle or giving, yet it was the most perfect act because in that moment it was exactly what they both wanted, both needed, engaging the senses in a totally spontaneous response to the emotional clamour of their bodies. It was the completion that his body had been demanding since that split-second connection in a restaurant three years earlier and he knew that nothing would ever surpass the exultation he felt as he plunged deep into her, compete with the stinging excitement of her nails biting into his shoulders, driving him on. Knowing that her passion equalled his as she clasped him against her, crying out as he brought her to release, burying her face into his shoulder, her lips into his neck as with a roar of triumph, he spilled into her. Made her his. Became hers in every way that it was possible for a man to be possessed by a woman.

He had always known that she was the one woman in the world who could make him lose his mind. She had just proved that beyond a doubt. And, while he held her, kept her close, her hair against his cheek, his lips against her hair, he thought reason well lost. While she clung to him as he wrapped her in the protective afterglow of tenderness, he could hope.

And when she finally lifted her head, her eyes huge and shining with the aftermath of love, her mouth invitingly soft, he had one sweet moment when he was certain that hope had been fulfilled.

But then he saw that the shine was not love, but tears.

He had been right. She wouldn't forget this moment in a hurry. Nor would he. But for all the wrong reasons.

He eased back, releasing her from the hard grip of the wall, supporting her as she lowered her feet, found her balance. Searching for some words, any words, as she pulled her clothes about her, straightened her skirt, all the time with an unceasing, silent stream of tears tearing at his heart. There were no words to convey his regret, his shame.

To say that he was sorry would insult her.

To tell her that he'd never intended it to happen would sound like so many empty words. She had just threatened to annul their marriage. His response could only be taken one way. And that was the charitable interpretation.

The other was that he had simply decided that, despite his fine words, his promises, he expected payment in full for his investment in an unwanted high-maintenance wife. Why else would he be planning to move into her home when, as she had just discovered, there was no need?

How could he ask her to forgive him, when he wouldn't be able to forgive himself?

Instead he picked up her jacket, handed it to her in silence.

'Bathroom?' she enquired, so quietly that he could barely hear her.

'Through here.' He opened the door to his bedroom and the untouched bed, just yards away, seemed to mock him. 'You'll find everything you'll need.'

Soap, hot water to wash him from her body.

She ducked through the opening, leaving him to straighten himself out. Consider a future that was suddenly bleaker than he could have imagined even a week ago. An hour ago. Then he'd had some hope.

He began to fasten his shirt, discovered that several of the buttons were torn from it, and dug a fresh one out of his holdall. On the point of balling up the discarded one and tossing it into the bin, he stopped, held it to his face, breathed in her scent for a moment, before folding it and putting it in the bag.

Fran didn't undress or take a shower. If she undressed she'd have to put the same clothes back on and she wasn't going to do that ever again. They were going into the bin the moment she got home. From the Jasper Conran suit to the Manolo Blahnik shoes she'd been wearing while she'd thrown herself at Guy like a whore. Her only consolation was that he could never call her 'cheap'.

Instead she splashed cold water on to her face. Washed her hands. Pulled out the pins that were falling out all around her and, since she hadn't got her bag with her, shook her hair loose. Then regarded herself in the mirror.

Her lips were bruised and swollen, her eyes bright and dark. One of the buttons on her jacket had been torn off and she had a rip in her stockings. She looked exactly what he must think she was.

A woman who'd come close to throwing away the soft option in a fit of pique. And had used the oldest trick in the book to save herself.

It hadn't been that way. It had been as if she'd stepped back in time to the moment she'd first seen him and recognised the moment for what it was. A *coup de foudre*, a lightning strike, a split second in which she'd known that he was the only man in the world for her, the one man she could never have. Only now there was nothing to hold her back, and all that pent up yearning, desire, had been loosed in a frenzied outburst of passion. Uncontrolled. Glorious in its absolute truth. Inexplicable unless the response was mutual.

But even if she couldn't explain, she would have to face him. The sooner the better.

She found him in the kitchen, slumped over the table, his face resting on his hands as he stared into space, as if into the jaws of hell.

'Guy? Are you all right?'

'What?' He started, looked at her.

'Can I get you something?'

'Oh, no. I really do have to go, but help yourself. Take your time…'

'We've already had this argument, Guy,' she said. 'I'm taking you to the airport, so if you have to go, let's do it.'

'Fran…' She'd loved the way he always called her Francesca. Her whole name. Soft and low. Suddenly she was reduced to Fran.

'Don't! Please, Guy. Don't... Don't say a word.' *Please don't say that you're sorry.* 'It happened. Let's just forget it.' For a moment their eyes locked and she knew he was as shocked, as overcome, as she was. And undoubtedly hating himself for betraying Steve's memory. 'Please.'

'If that's what you want.' Then, rising to his feet, 'Let's go.'

Which more or less put a stop to any attempt at communication, beyond the banal. The heavy traffic. The chance of rain. It was worse than silence, Fran thought. She wanted to say so much. Couldn't say any of it. He'd married her out of duty. Guilt. Because it was the last wish of a brother he felt he'd let down. He hadn't counted on getting some sex-starved female flinging herself at him at the first opportunity.

And when he'd pulled up in the drop zone at the airport and she'd climbed out so that she could take his place in the driving seat while he took his bag from the boot, all she could say was, 'You will take care of yourself, Guy? Don't do anything stupid, will you?'

He glanced at her sideways. 'It's a bit late for that, wouldn't you say?'

'That's not—'

'I know.' He dragged his fingers through his hair. 'I'm sorry.'

She shook her head. 'Guy, about Toby...'

'He's your son. Nothing can happen without your agreement. When I said—'

'I was going to say that he'll miss you,' she said. *I'll miss you.* 'Don't let what happened... Just don't stay away because of that.'

'I'll miss him too,' he said. But not making any

promises. 'If you have any problems, need anything, just call my office or go and see Tom. He'll look after you.'

'Who'll look after you, Guy?'

'Me? I don't need anyone to take care of me.'

'No, I mean it. It's dangerous out there. Do you really have to go?'

He reached out as if to touch her cheek, then, as if remembering what had happened the last time he'd done that, he thought better of it and curled his fingers tight against his palm before picking up his bag. But her cheek remembered his touch and her body responded to the memory.

'If you need to get a message to me the office will know how to get hold of me.'

'Your sensational secretary?'

'The very same.' Then, before she could reply, he walked away and, as the automatic doors swished open, disappeared into the mêlée of the departure hall.

'Guy!' she called desperately. But too late. The doors had already closed behind him and as she made a move to follow she saw a traffic warden looking pointedly at the car.

'You can't leave that there, miss. It'll be towed away.'

'But...' But what? 'No. I'm just going.'

It was probably just as well. What would she have said to him anyway? I love you?

Not under these circumstances. After today he wouldn't want to hear her say it under any circumstances.

CHAPTER NINE

FRAN felt as if she was grieving all over again.

She'd pulled into the garage and finally given way to the dammed-up tears she hadn't been able to shed for Steven in a mind-clearing storm of guilt and loss. And when it was over she finally understood it all. That their marriage of convenience had been entirely for his expedience, not hers.

Not cheap. But then this wasn't about money. It was about control. Toby was all the family he had. His heir. The boy who carried the family name. Marriage was the simplest and most effective way of stopping her from becoming involved with someone else, giving him some other man's name.

Which answered any question she had about what was in the letter Steven had written to him. He had been a less than perfect partner, a less than perfect anything, except father. Relaxed to the point of being comatose on most things, he had been uncharacteristically firm in his insistence that Dymoke be added to Toby's name.

Too late she saw that all that stuff about inheritance tax had been so much wool being pulled over her eyes. Guy had bought the house to keep her in place, and while she was still reeling from shock, still confused enough not to be able to think things through clearly, he'd rushed her through the marriage ceremony.

There had been nothing altruistic about any of it.

He was even converting the top floor of the house into an apartment for himself. Moving himself into their lives...

And the sex? Had that been planned too?

She shook her head, trying to clear it...

She hadn't been thinking straight. The wedding had upset her and then she'd realised that his apartment wasn't the sterile environment that he'd led her to believe, lacking the emotional warmth of a home, but a carefully, lovingly prepared setting for the woman he'd hoped would share it with him. Her presence had been so strong in the room that she'd almost felt her...

At that moment she'd been hurting so much that she'd have said, done, almost anything to wound him. But then he'd looked at her...

He'd never taken a woman like that. Without thought, control, consideration of the consequences.

Never before had he experienced that kind of no-holds-barred response. It had made him feel invincible. Made him shake with need...

But the fact that she'd been an eager and willing partner, matching his own need with a breathless urgency and heat that had swept away any thought of restraint, excused nothing. He had taken on himself a duty of care. She'd been distraught, upset, vulnerable, but when she'd looked up at him all of that had been blown away. She had looked at him as if... As if...

He cut off the pitiful tricks of his subconscious. There was no excuse. What did it matter how she'd looked at him? He'd not only betrayed her, but everything he stood for.

Bad enough to lose it so completely, but he'd left

her without a word of apology, of explanation. But what else could he have done? Tell her truth? Tell her that he loved her?

She'd made it plain enough she didn't want to hear his pitiful apologies. All she'd wanted was to get him out of her life.

He had thought he'd known what it was to be alone. He hadn't begun to imagine the emptiness...

'Fran?'

It seemed like hours later when Matty's voice broke through the pain and she gathered herself, looked at her watch. She didn't know what time Guy's flight left. He'd probably already taken off. Been glad to go.

She wished she hadn't let him leave that way, had let him say what was on his mind no matter how painful the words might have been. She should have had the courage to confront him, confront her own weakness.

But regret was just a waste of time.

She had to think of the future, grasp the chance to make something of the business Steven had left her. Make something of herself. If Guy saw that she was not just some pathetic female who needed a man to look after her he might, one day, look at her like that again...

'Fran, what's happened? Where's Guy?'

'He's gone,' she said.

'But he'll be coming back?'

'Yes, he'll be coming back.' And she climbed out of the car and held out her hand with the tell-tale ring still fastened immovably to her finger.

'Oh, my dear. What have you done?'

She told her exactly what she'd done. And why. All of it. The whole truth, and when she'd finished Matty just hugged her. There was nothing else she could do or say.

Not that she had time to dwell on what had happened. She had the business to keep her occupied. And the weekly calls from the 'sensational' Catherine who, no doubt, had instructions to check that she had everything she needed—just in case the credit cards weren't enough—and that the builders were getting on with the job. To ensure that she hadn't taken his money and disappeared with her son... His heir...

And, as the weeks lengthened into months, to despatch gifts for Christmas for all of them. Even Connie was not forgotten, squealing with delight as she unwrapped the handbag that had been gift-wrapped and delivered by a top-people's store.

He'd sent her a book. A biography of the woman she'd once told him that she admired, aspired to be like. It was an obvious choice, top of the bestseller list, and she tried not to fool herself into believing he'd picked it out himself.

And, as winter retreated and the first daffodils began to appear, Catherine's calls had the added comfort of reassuring her that he was safe in the terrifying country that seemed to have swallowed him up so completely he might have disappeared off the face of the earth.

It was nearly Easter when, sitting glued to the early-evening news, watching pictures of riots, the reports of civil unrest that seemed worse with every passing week, she heard the doorbell rang. She left it for

Connie to answer, only looking up when the sitting room door opened.

A tall fair-haired woman hesitated on the threshold. 'Your housekeeper said it was all right to come through…' And when she still didn't speak, 'I can't believe we haven't met already. I feel as if I know you so well.'

'Catherine?' She recognised the voice, but the reality did not match the picture in her imagination. Tall, blonde… And old enough to be her mother.

'Can I come in?'

Realising that she was staring open-mouthed, she scrambled to her feet. 'I'm so sorry,' she said, taking the proffered hand. 'I was miles away…'

'Watching the news. It's not good, is it?'

Fran's heart gave a wild leap of fear. 'Is that why you've come? To tell me—'

'No, no. I'm sorry. I didn't mean to give you a fright. I've just come to bring you something. Well, for your little boy. I just thought that perhaps you should have the opportunity to veto it first. Is he around? Toby?'

'No, he's downstairs with Matty.'

'In that case I'll go and fetch it from the car.'

She returned a few moments later with a cardboard box that she placed on the floor and when she opened it the small silky brown and white head of a spaniel puppy appeared. Then a body wriggled free of the blanket and he looked up at her and whined to be lifted out.

She was lost for words. Guy might have left Catherine to pick out Christmas gifts, but this could only have come direct from him. Proof that he was thinking of her... She caught herself. Thinking of Toby.

'I made the woman at the kennels promise she'd take him back if you didn't want him. Men have these great ideas...'

'When? When did Guy ask you to do this?'

'Oh, months ago. In fact, I think he called from the airport... It was supposed to have been Toby's Christmas present, but since he was so particular it had to wait until the right spaniel produced the right pup.' She shrugged apologetically. 'You know Guy. He's never satisfied with less than perfection.'

'No?' Her heart lurched uncomfortably. 'No,' she agreed.

'The puppy had to be from a private breeder he'd chosen. And it had to be brown and white. And male.'

'Yes. He'd want that.' And when Catherine lifted her eyebrows. 'Steven had a puppy like this when he was a boy.'

'Oh, I see. I wondered...' Then, when she didn't—couldn't—say anything, 'Unfortunately, the mummy dog wasn't on the same schedule as Santa. Anyway, the breeder is happy to take him back if this is a less than thrilling surprise,' Catherine said, clearly assuming that her shocked reaction was horror at this unexpected arrival. 'Men have these great ideas, bless them, but they don't have to deal with the puddles. Or the walks. I speak from experience here...'

'No. He's perfect,' Fran said, kneeling down to rub the pup's head with her fingertips. 'Hello, Harry Two.' Then, when he whined to be picked up, 'Oh, no. You're not mine. Toby gets first cuddle.' And she tucked him carefully back in the basket with the blanket around him before turning to Catherine. 'Want to see a little boy's face light up?'

Half an hour later, looking on at boy and puppy lost in mutual admiration, Catherine said, 'This is so what Guy needs. A family to come home to. All he's done the past few years is fieldwork but it's a young man's game. Have the builders actually started work on the alterations yet?'

'No, not yet,' Fran said. 'The architect is having to sort out the retrospective planning permission for the extension, which is slowing everything down.'

Thank goodness.

'But the interior designer came to see you? About the redecoration of your bedroom?'

'Oh, yes. God bless him,' Fran said.

'He's that good?'

'Oh, he's great, but it isn't that. The sweet man nearly wet himself with excitement when he saw a hideous frog I'd brought home from the warehouse to prop open the garage door. Made an offer for the lot on the spot. And then bought a truckload of equally unattractive lamps when he came to the warehouse to collect them. I thought I was going to have to pay someone to take them away when I moved out of Steven's offices.'

'How's the business going? I saw that Christmas piece in the *Courier* last November, featuring your fabulous silk wrappers,' she said. 'Great PR, by the way. I did all my gift shopping with one phone call.'

'I was lucky. I sent the editor a wrapper and she came to see me, make sure I was for real, and she fell in love with them. She's doing a feature on me next week. You know the kind of thing. Plucky-mother-runs-business-from-her-attic... Happily, it coincides with the arrival of the new summer-weight wrappers and some totally gorgeous matching pyjamas. I couldn't afford that kind of advertising.'

'I was going to ask if you had anything new. It always seems to be someone's birthday…'

'I went out to China in January and talked to the cooperative who make this stuff—'

'On your own?'

Who else was there? She'd been scared witless, but she'd had to do it. As Guy had said, there were things you couldn't send anyone else to do. And she'd been welcomed so warmly. Treated with such respect…

'I needed to go myself.'

'Yes, but surely in your—'

'Did you mention any of this to Guy? About the company, I mean?'

'It's not my business, Fran. I'm just a messenger.'

Which was a tactful way of saying that he never asked about her, Fran thought. Didn't want to know.

'Do you want me to tell him?' Catherine prompted.

'Oh, no,' she said. Then laughed as if it wasn't important. As if she didn't want to astound him with her brilliance when he finally got home. 'He's got more than enough to worry about, I should think.'

'In that case I imagine you'd rather I didn't mention that you're expecting a baby.'

Guy wiped the sweat from his eyes with his sleeve, booted up the laptop and downloaded his report via the satellite uplink. Checked to see if there were any messages from the office. The one from Tom Palmer with an attachment leapt out at him. It was as if he'd been holding his breath, waiting for it. But it wasn't the formal application for an annulment he'd been anticipating for months.

It was an article about Francesca in the *Courier*. About the success of her fledgling mail order business. As he read it he found himself hearing her voice as he read her words. Filled with joy as he looked at her adored face, delighted with her success.

The camera had caught her as she'd swirled around in a loose silk wrapper, throwing her head back, laughing, looking wonderful.

She'd put back the weight she'd lost. Her hair was a deeper colour. She looked exactly as she had that moment he'd first...

No.

He rose to his feet, fighting for breath.

Not exactly the way she had looked then. On that occasion her pregnancy hadn't shown. This time, although disguised by the loose wrap, he could see that it was well advanced. He didn't need to guess how well advanced. He knew exactly how many months, days, hours it was since he'd held her, given her the child she was carrying.

Every day since he'd left her he'd had to fight the urge to go back. Punishing himself. But his feelings no longer mattered. He had to get back. Had to be there for her. With her. Giving her his emotional as well as his financial support. He refused to listen to the voice in his head warning him that she wouldn't want him. She needed him and he would take whatever she hurled at him by way of accusation, anger, abuse. And this time nothing would stop him from telling her the way he felt about her, the entire truth from beginning to end. Tell her and keep telling her until she believed him.

'Fran, are you watching the news?'

It was late and, deep in thought, she'd picked up the phone on automatic. 'Oh, Matty... No, I'm trying to decide whether we need to expand our range of goods.' The lightly quilted wrappers had been joined by a summer-weight companion—pyjamas, jewel-rich scarves and some little silk embroidered boxes which she knew were going to be a huge hit. 'I've been offered some rather special scented candles to match our colour range and I've really got to max-imise the cost-return on this catalogue—'

'Shut up, Fran! It's Guy, he's on the television...' She didn't hear the rest of the sentence, dropping the phone as she reached for the remote, flicking desper-ately through the channels until she found one of the rolling news channels.

'...concerns for the missing geologist's where-abouts have grown since he left camp planning to travel to the capital last week and failed to arrive. Isolated rebel groups who have recently moved into the area have seized foreign nationals hostage in the past, using them to force concessions from the gov-ernment. Neither the Foreign Office nor Mr Dymoke's company would comment on whether any such demands—'

The doorbell began to ring. A long, urgent blast that sent her flying to the door. It was Catherine.

'Tell me,' she demanded.

'I tried to get to you before the damned news...'

'Tell me, Catherine!'

'I don't know. He wasn't due to come home for

another six weeks but he sent an urgent e-mail telling me to book him a flight and apparently left camp straight afterwards. He never arrived…'

Fran sank on to the bottom of the stairs. 'I begged him not to go.'

Catherine joined her, putting her arms around her. 'It'll be all right. He's tough as old boots.'

'He's not bullet-proof.'

'He's no use to anyone dead, Fran. If the rebels have him they'll want to negotiate.'

'And how long will that take?' Months. Years. 'What the hell is he doing there risking his life?' Then, 'I wish I'd told him about the baby. I wish I'd told him that I love him.' She looked at Catherine, pleading for understanding. 'I should have told him that I love him…'

The sound of the stair-lift announced the arrival of Matty. She took one look at them and said, 'I'll go and make some tea.'

'Tea? Where's your bottle of Scotch when we need it?'

'Safely downstairs where it won't play havoc with your blood pressure. Go and put your feet up—'

'Don't treat me like an invalid!' The phone began to ring and she leapt up before Catherine could beat her to it and snatched it up. 'What?'

'Francesca…'

'Guy…'

She could scarcely hear him, his voice breaking up, too distorted to be recognised. But it had to be him. No one else called her Francesca. It was the one word that came through whole and unbroken as the poor connection stuttered and hissed so that all she caught were fragments that she had to guess at.

'Okay… Home…'

Words that tortured her and she cut them short. 'Guy, I don't know what the devil you're saying so stop wasting time talking and get back here! Right now! Do you hear me?'

And then there was nothing. Only an echoing silence. Had he hung up? She stared at the phone in horror.

'That was Guy? Is he okay?' Matty demanded. 'What did he say?'

'He rang me…'

'Who else would he ring, idiot…?' Catherine was grinning. Why was she grinning?

'I don't believe it. He rang me and I shouted at him. How could I do that? I was going to tell him that I love him…'

For two days she wouldn't go out, but remained glued to the television. Never moved out of reach of a telephone. Waiting for him to call again. Waiting for news. There was plenty of it, but most of it was confused, contradictory. He was still a prisoner. The rescue helicopter had been brought down. He had never been kidnapped but was simply lost somewhere. He'd been shot—

All she had to hang on to was his voice, her name in the ether…

'Fran?' She looked round. 'We're going now,' Connie said. 'You going to be all right?'

'Going?'

'Toby has a birthday party with his friend.'

'Oh, yes…' She forced herself away from the television. 'Yes, of course. I'd forgotten. Have you got money for the taxi? A present? You'll be good, Toby, won't you? Remember to say thank you.'

'Maybe you should go,' Connie muttered darkly. 'Baby could do with a change of scene.'

Baby needs his daddy, she thought, looking back at the television.

'We'll be home about six.'

'Have a good time,' she said. Then, 'Damn!' as the front door slammed shut.

Angry with herself, she turned off the television, got to her feet. Guy might not be rescued for months. Was she planning on spending every hour in front of the television in case there was the slightest snippet of news? It was the last thing he'd want. Catherine would let her know the minute anyone heard anything and in the meantime there were a hundred things that needed doing. She still hadn't settled on the final lay-out for the slender catalogue that was going to be mailed out to all their customers, as well put as an insert in one of the Sunday supplements.

It was going to cost a fortune. It had to be right.

She caught sight of herself in the hall mirror. What a wreck. She needed to take a shower, wash her hair, change. Get her mind back on the job. On her family…

But when she opened a drawer, searching for underwear that would stretch around her expanding belly, she found herself staring at the tiny silk box that contained the wedding ring Guy had put on her finger and she opened it.

The simple circle of gold gleamed rich and warm and she picked it up, slipped it on to her finger, felt…comforted. As if he were closer. And, instead of working on her catalogue, she went across to the

newly decorated master bedroom where the few pos-
sessions he'd packed up and removed from the apartment had been placed, waiting to be unpacked.

She opened a large, old-fashioned leather trunk and
began putting away his things. Shirts. Sweaters. Suits.
She lifted up the sleeve of the one he'd worn at their
wedding, touching it to her cheek.

Put his shoes on the racks. His socks and his underwear in drawers.

An affirmation that he would soon be home.

The box contained sealed packets of personal papers and she stored them in the lowboy. Then took
out a large padded envelope that had been sent to
Steven. Opened. Marked 'Return to Sender'. And
nothing on earth could have stopped her from looking
inside.

She stared at the silver rattle for a long time. Guy
had sent Steven this family treasure for Toby. And
Steven had returned it. He hadn't wanted to let his
brother back into their lives.

Why?

She finally put it to one side, finished emptying the
box. Took out the few books he'd brought with him,
placing them beside the bed. A piece of paper flut-
tered out of one of them and as she bent to pick it up
she recognised the writing.

Steven's letter. She sank on to the edge of the bed,
holding it in both hands, knowing that it was private.
Knowing that it held all the answers…

She was still staring at it when the doorbell rang.
It would be Catherine. She had said she'd drop by
after work. She hadn't realised it was so late and
glanced at her watch. It wasn't…

And then she knew. Was running down the stairs,

fumbling with the door, but when she flung it open there was no one on the step and for a moment she was utterly confused.

Had she imagined it? She stepped outside to look up and down the street but there was no one about, only someone paying off a taxi that had stopped a few yards away. His hair was long and unkempt. His beard days old. His clothes past saving. He didn't look as if he could have afforded the price of a bus ticket, let alone a taxi. And then as he turned, looked up, she saw his face. The cut roughly stitched over his right eye, his cheek bone bruised black, his arm in a makeshift sling…

Guy.

Shock took her breath away. She struggled for air so that she could say his name. Say the words that were rushing in a torrent to get out. But as she walked slowly down the steps to meet him, his gaze dropped from her face to her burgeoning stomach, to where the baby they'd made in an explosive moment of passion lay beneath her heart.

Guy was exhausted, aching in every limb, but as he saw the woman he loved standing in the lamplight he felt a surge of something so powerful that he could have taken on the world. He felt such overwhelming gratitude that she hadn't rushed for the morning after pill. He could not have blamed her…

Choked, all he could do was smile stupidly and say, 'I really buggered up your plans for an annulment, didn't I?'

For a moment Francesca thought her heart might break. Was that all it meant to him?

She'd kept his baby when Matty had tactfully suggested the morning after pill. Protected it against the raised eyebrows of neighbours, the gossip of Steven's friends. Cherished it with her love and hope for the future and all it meant to him was that he had stopped her from ending their marriage.

Then, as she saw the tears glinting in his eyes, she realised that she had been wrong. That he was simply protecting himself from hurt, from rejection. That somehow he'd found out and rushed back to her. And she finally understood the few words of Steven's letter that she'd read before the ring on the doorbell had her racing down the stairs.

…when I walked in behind her you were lit up…

It had not been an illusion. That split second of mutual recognition when their eyes had met…

It was why he'd gone away. Why Steven had returned the rattle. If he'd shown it to her she'd have written to thank him and Steven didn't want her even that close to his brother.

It had happened again in his apartment. It was as if they had both been locked in that moment for the last three years, holding their breath, waiting for the completion of a connection that could only have one outcome.

And she reached out, took his undamaged hand in hers and placed it on the baby growing inside her, holding it there with her own so that he could feel the life they'd created kicking strongly. See his ring gleaming softly in the light spilling down from the street lamp.

'It's all right, Guy,' she said. 'It's all right. I know.'

And she reached out for him, drew him close, pressed her cheek against his. Kissed him.

His mouth was cold and for one terrible moment she thought she had it all wrong as he pulled away to stare down at her. Then, with a desperate cry that broke the silence, he called out her name and caught her to him, kissing her until she thought she would turn to liquid heat, crushing her to him so that she felt his tears mingle with her own.

'You going to stand out here in the street kissing like kids all night? Letting in the cold?'

He broke away, but his eyes never left hers as he said, 'Hello, Connie. I've missed your cooking.'

'Don't you "Hello, Connie" me. Where you been, eh? Worrying Fran half to death...'

'Were you?' he asked. 'Worried? You didn't fancy being a rich widow?' Maybe he already knew the answer because he didn't wait for it but looked down and said, 'Hello, Toby. Been to a party?'

'Mmm.' He gave Connie the balloon he was holding and offered up his goodie bag. 'I've got cake.'

'Any to spare? I'm starving...'

'Later. It's bath time,' Fran said. 'Can you take care of Toby for me, Connie?'

'I can take care of both of them if you like,' she offered. 'He's going to need help with his arm in plaster. No? You don't want Connie?' And she went inside chuckling to herself. 'Just you make sure you wash behind his ears, Fran.' Then, 'I call Matty and tell her Mr Guy is home.'

'What do you want first? Drink? Food? Bath?'

He circled her with his arm as they walked up the steps into the house. 'I've got everything I want right here, my love. Absolutely everything.'

'My love?'

'I've waited too long to tell you.'

'No. Before would have been too soon. Today is just right.'

'You believe me? I thought I'd have to keep telling you for the next ten years before I managed to convince you.'

'Oh, I'll expect you to go on telling me for longer than that. A whole lifetime more. But right now you should have a bath, and while you're soaking you can tell me exactly what happened to you.'

'Tom Palmer sent me an e-mail,' he said a few minutes later, as he lay back, relaxing in the warmth of the newly decorated bathroom. 'I thought it was about the annulment—I'd been expecting it for months. But it was an article with a photograph of an amazing young woman who was running a business out of her attic. A very pregnant young woman.'

'Oh.'

'I thought… I don't know what I thought… I just knew I had to get home. To be here for you. Help. Do anything. Everything. Except go away. Why didn't you tell me, Fran?'

'How could I tell you when I didn't know how you felt? I wanted you to come home but not out of guilt. I wanted you to come home because nothing would keep you away.'

'You think I didn't want to? Words can't describe how much I yearned to be here with you. I thought you hated me. I'd given you every reason—'

'I know. I know why you did it.' She knelt down beside the bath, took his hand, lifted it to her lips. 'I was beginning to wonder if I'd have to absolve Catherine from the promise I extracted from her…'

'Thank goodness you didn't get at Tom. I've never packed up a camp so fast, but by the time I left it was dark and raining stair-rods. Of course I was driving like a complete maniac and didn't see the road had been washed out until it was too late. Fortunately some villagers found me, took me to the nearest clinic to be patched up, but communication was a bit.hit and miss.' Then, 'But I did get the message.'

'Message?'

'What was it? Something along the lines of "…get back here. Right now…" Very forceful.'

'Oh, *that* message.' She grinned for a moment. Then, more seriously, 'I didn't mean to shout at you but you were all over the news as missing, kidnapped, shot… I was so scared. So desperate. I meant to tell you then how much I love you…' Then, when she saw him grinning, 'And, by the way, you're staying home from now on. I don't care how important the project is, someone else can do it.'

A long time later, after he'd had a bath and a shave and they'd tucked Toby up in bed and they were curled up on the sofa, his arm around her, she said, 'Steven knew how you felt, didn't he?' She twisted around to look up at him. 'I found the rattle while I was unpacking your things earlier this evening. And his letter. I never had a chance to read it, but a couple of lines seemed to leap off the page at me…'

'Yes, he knew. When you burst through that door you caught me off-guard. If I'd had any idea what was coming I might have been ready…' Then, looking down at her he smiled, leaned forward to kiss her. 'No. I've been fooling myself. Nothing could have saved me…'

'You are getting better at the compliments.' Then she frowned. 'I think.'

'He had no idea that you were equally felled, if that helps. I didn't know myself.'

'He used it, didn't he? To drive you away.'

'He was afraid that he wouldn't be able to hold on to you. He was so insecure he thought that if I was there, if I wanted you…' He shook his head. 'He was wrong. I wouldn't have done anything to come between you. He didn't have to—'

'What?'

'Make me angry. I already knew I had to stay away. You were having his child. Whatever I felt, in the face of that, was completely irrelevant. And I was right. If he hadn't died, you'd have married him.'

'He loved me, Guy. He was a good father.'

'I'm glad he was happy.'

'And that he had the good sense to leave me to you. In his will. Give you a second chance.'

Guy didn't disillusion her. Instead he said, 'Oh, right. And what would you have done if I'd come home demanding to move into my non-existent attic flat?'

'You don't need a flat, Guy. I, on the other hand, had to cut overheads to the minimum when the bank refused to back me and the top floor is the perfect place. Just big enough for Claire and Jason and me.'

'Don't you need a warehouse? Thousands of people answering the phones and despatching the goods?'

'I outsourced that to a call centre and a warehouse facility. We just do the buying and the marketing.'

'It couldn't have been easy.'

'It wasn't, but then nothing worthwhile ever is.' Then, 'Anyway, forget business and forget the flat. The master suite has been redecorated just for you. I know it's not quite what you had in mind but it's very comfortable—'

'It's perfect, Francesca. But I'm done with our marriage of convenience. Unless you come with it—'

'I thought I already had,' she said, grinning up at him wickedly.

'—until death us do part,' he went on, although his voice wasn't quite so steady, 'I'd rather take my chances with pushing together two desks in the attic.'

'Guy, when I made that vow in front of the registrar and those two sweet ladies who were our witnesses, I meant it. That was why it was so difficult for me when I thought you were simply doing what you saw as your duty.'

'Is that what you thought?' And, taking her hand, he slipped the wedding ring from her finger, tilting it to show her the inscription engraved inside. There was just one word.

Forever.

Fran caught her breath. 'I didn't know,' she began. 'I didn't see…'

'I wanted it written somewhere, even if I was the only person in the world who would ever know.' Then, 'Would you like to do it again? Properly?'

'I'm sorry?'

'In church, with a big dress, a vintage Rolls and a reception in a marquee in the garden with everyone we care about around us.'

'You mean a blessing?' She couldn't keep the smile from breaking out all over her face. 'That is the most beautiful…' For a moment she thought she was going to cry again, but this time from sheer happiness. Then, 'But there's just one condition.' He waited. 'If

I'm going to wear the big occasion dress, I'd like to wait until it's only the dress that's big…'

The Saturday after the baptism of Stephanie Joy Dymoke, her mother and father made eternal vows to love, honour and keep one another in sickness and in health for all their days.

Matty, her wheelchair decorated with white and silver ribbons, held her little god-daughter throughout the service.

Toby performed valiantly as ring-bearer.

Connie wept buckets and told everyone who would listen that Francesca was the kindest, most wonderful woman on earth and Guy kissed her and told her that she was absolutely right.

The marquee was a picture in yellow and white, and after lunch and a great many toasts Guy took Francesca's hand and took the first turn around the dance floor to the applause of family and friends.

'Do you realise that this is the first time we've danced together?' she said.

'We have a whole lifetime of firsts ahead of us, my love. Our first honeymoon—'

'You can only have one proper honeymoon,' she objected.

'True, but once you've got the hang of it you can have endless improper ones.'

She giggled, then said, 'Our first family holiday—'

'By the sea. Rock pools and sandcastles and paddling.'

'Toby will love it. And so will Harry Two.' Then, 'Our first Christmas together. Trimming the tree, buying presents—'

'Toby's first day at school—'

'And before we know it he'll be our first sulky
teenager—'

'Producing our first grandchild—'

She laughed. 'Okay, you win. I really don't want
to go any further than that.'

He stopped. 'You do know that I love you so much
that I can hardly bear it, Francesca Lang?'

She knew, and she'd told him a thousand times,
shown him in a thousand ways, how much she loved
him. All but one. And now was the time.

'Not Lang,' she said. 'Dymoke. I want the whole
world to know that I'm your wife; "...from this day
forward..." I am Mrs Guy Dymoke.' And then, just
to be sure that everyone had got the message, she put
her arms around his neck and kissed him.

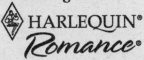
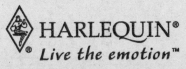

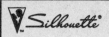

INTIMATE MOMENTS™

presents a provocative new miniseries by
award-winning author

INGRID WEAVER

PAYBACK

Three rebels were brought back from the brink and
recruited into the shadowy Payback Organization.
In return for this extraordinary second chance, they
must each repay one favor in the future. But if they
renege on their promise, everything that matters
will be ripped away...including love!

Available in March 2005:

The Angel and the Outlaw
(IM #1352)

Hayley Tavistock will do anything to avenge the
murder of her brother—including forming an
uneasy alliance with gruff ex-con Cooper Webb.
With the walls closing in around them, can love
defy the odds?

Watch for Book #2 in June 2005...

Loving the Lone Wolf
(IM #1370)

Available at your favorite retail outlet.

The world's bestselling romance series.

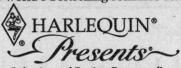

HARLEQUIN® *Presents*

Seduction and Passion Guaranteed!

Legally wed, but he's never said...
"I love you."

They're...

Wedlocked!

The series
where
marriages are
made in haste...
and love
comes later...

**Look out for more Wedlocked! marriage stories in
Harlequin Presents throughout 2005**

Coming in March:
HIS BRIDE FOR ONE NIGHT by Miranda Lee, #2451

Coming in April:
THE BILLION-DOLLAR BRIDE by Kay Thorpe, #2462

Coming in May:
THE DISOBEDIENT BRIDE by Helen Bianchin, #2463

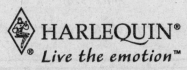

HARLEQUIN®
Live the emotion™

If you enjoyed what you just read,
then we've got an offer you can't resist!

Take 2 bestselling
love stories FREE!

Plus get a FREE surprise gift!

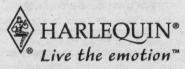

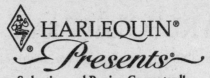